TROWBRIDGE ROAD

TROWBRIDGE ROAD

MARCELLA PIXLEY

CANDLEWICK PRESS

Copyright © 2020 by Marcella Pixley

First edition 2020

Library of Congress Catalog Card Number pending
ISBN 978-1-5362-0750-7

20 21 22 23 24 25 LBM 10 9 8 7 6 5 4 3 2 1

Printed in Melrose Park, IL, U.S.A.

This book was typeset in Dante MT.

Candlewick Press
99 Dover Street
Somerville, Massachusetts 02144

visit us at www.candlewick.com

A JUNIOR LIBRARY GUILD SELECTION

To my mother, Jacqueline Fleischman,
who loved this book
before it even drew its first breath

Something New

———

It was clear that the summer was about to change as soon as Jenny Karlo's rusty old Chevy came clattering down Trowbridge Road at a quarter past two, the radio pounding heavy metal into the neighborhood, shattering the lazy Thursday afternoon like a rock through a dusty window.

When the door creaked open and Jenny stepped onto the cracked sidewalk with her black high-heeled boots, her bare legs, and her feathered red hair down past her shoulders, it seemed like the maple trees and the tall Victorian houses leaned in, not because they were leering at her like so many of the fathers did, but because something about Jenny changed everything that came close to her.

She took a drag on her cigarette.

"Get out of the car, Ziggy," she said.

The back door opened, but the boy did not emerge.

"You need me to go back there and pull you?"

"No," muttered the boy. "I can do it."

He unfolded from the backseat, a beanpole in green-striped jogging shorts and a purple *Return of the Jedi* T-shirt. He had an unruly mop of long red hair down his back and a white ferret perched on his shoulder, snuffling at the wind.

He joined Jenny on the sidewalk. They stood side by side and looked up at the house. The boy reached for his mother's hand. Hers were already occupied. One was holding the cigarette, and the other was hooked into the back pocket of her cutoff jeans. His hand flopped empty back down to his side.

"You got your stuff?" asked Jenny.

Ziggy nodded and lifted a battered suitcase with one shrugged shoulder.

"Okay, then. Let's go."

They walked together across the flagstones and then up the wooden steps.

Nana Jean swung open the door before they knocked. She made a strange sound—some kind of mixture between happy and sad, a sound that only a grandmother can make—and pulled Ziggy toward her. "It's the right thing," she said over his shoulder. "Oh, Jenny, Jenny, I know this is hard, but it's the right thing. You'll see."

"Well, okay. It's the right thing. Let's hurry up before I change my mind."

"We'll stay in touch," said Nana Jean breathlessly, rubbing the boy's back. "I already made arrangements, and he can start school here with the other kids at the end of the summer, no problem. He'll like it in Newton. No more bullies. No more teasing. Everything's going to be just fine now. I'll take really good care of him, Jenny. You hear me?"

"Yeah," said Jenny. "I hear you. And I appreciate that. I really do. It sure has been a tough year."

"I know," said Nana Jean. "Let me worry about Ziggy, and you just work on getting yourself well. One day at a time. Right? Isn't that what they say?"

"That's what they say," said Jenny.

She took one more drag on the cigarette, blew

smoke over her shoulder, dropped the butt on the porch, and stamped it out with the heel of her boot.

The white ferret climbed down from the boy's shoulder. Then it scrambled onto the porch, grabbed the butt in one claw, and started gnawing at it.

Nana Jean and Jenny both looked at the ferret because it was easier than looking at each other.

"Well, okay, Ziggy," said Jenny. "You be good for Nana Jean. And don't let that creature sleep in your pants. You hear me?" She took the boy by the shoulders and pulled him away from his grandmother. "Animals aren't meant to sleep in people's pants," she said. "It's disgusting. And it ruins them. Ferrets smell like skunk, you know. And clothes are expensive. Money doesn't grow on trees, even here in Newton Highlands."

"But Matthew likes being close to me," said Ziggy. "He likes my scent." Ziggy scooped the ferret from the ground, kissed him on the top of his white head, and then grinned at the creature. The ferret licked his teeth, his white tail twitching.

"Well, now," said Nana Jean, pulling the ferret from Ziggy's mouth and holding him in front of her like a dirty rag. "First things first. Let's see what we can do to get you two settled in. I've got Jenny's old room all ready, and I want you and Matthew to sleep any way that feels comfortable. If he wants to sleep in your pants, it's okay with me as long as you're *out* of them when he does it. No sleepless nights in Nana's house. Nobody's going to bother you anymore, Ziggy. Things are going to change now that Nana's taking care of you. You hear me?"

"Thank you, Nana," said Ziggy.

"Okay," said Jenny. "I think I'd better go now."

"Give him a kiss and tell him you love him," said Nana Jean.

Obediently, Jenny knelt on the porch in front of her gangly boy.

Ziggy kissed his mother's hair. "I love you, Jenny," he said.

Jenny closed her eyes and leaned against him.

"You be the Walrus, Goo Goo Boy," she said.

"I am," said Ziggy. "I am the Walrus."

Jenny got up from the ground. "Then give me a high slide," she said.

Jenny put her hand out, and Ziggy ran his index finger down the length of her palm. Then he snapped and pointed at her. He had tears streaming down his cheeks.

"He's the Walrus," said Jenny, smiling now with

tears in her eyes. "He's my Goo Goo Boy. No matter what happens."

Nana Jean took Ziggy by the hand. She opened the screen door and led him into the house.

Jenny stood alone on the porch. She watched the old house swallow them and looked out over Trowbridge Road at the row of houses with their closed doors. After a while, she sighed and made her way back to the car. She got in, lit another cigarette, rolled down the window, started the engine, cranked up the radio, and clattered down Trowbridge Road and on toward town.

Copper Beech

———◆———

The thickest branch of Nana Jean's copper beech tree was a perfect place to watch the neighborhood. From the ground, you could catch a glimpse here and there: The postman brought the mail. Mr. Moniker took out his garbage, bent forward to arrange the cans, and then hiked up his pants before shuffling back into his house.

From the tree, I saw the fullness of Trowbridge Road — all the normal things that take place without anyone noticing how beautiful they are. I could see the old hollow behind Nana Jean's house that used to be a farm a hundred years ago when Newton Highlands still had dairy cows. I could see Lucy and Heather Anne Delmato sun-tanning on their porch roof in matching hot-pink Day-Glo string bikinis, Lucy's boom box blasting that summer's top hits on the radio — Michael Jackson, Cyndi Lauper, people I always thought looked plastic on TV. I could see the Crowley boys at their house, riding their Huffy bikes over dirt piles, popping wheelies, and jeering at each other. I watched people pulling in and out of their driveways. Mrs. Koning, back from the supermarket with a paper bag filled with groceries. Mrs. Wright off to Crystal Lake for a swim. Mr. Lewis, back from the corner store with a sports magazine and a six-pack of Budweiser beer.

All the comings and goings of life.

Sometimes I imagined that my spying was the magic that tied Trowbridge Road to the world. I imagined that if I stopped watching for some reason, if I *stopped* noticing all the cars and all the grocery bags, and all the people opening and closing their car doors, everything in the world would come completely unhinged and swirl into a vacuum like Dorothy Gale's farm in the twister: the tractor, the cow, the shed, Uncle Henry and Auntie Em and the wicked old Miss Gulch on her bicycle, and everything.

After lunch, Nana Jean and Ziggy came back out to the porch and sat quietly, the old woman in the wicker chair, the boy on the concrete step, the ferret bouncing between them like a feather duster. Sometimes she pulled him close, and he sat there, stiff and unmoving, which made me so sad, I almost couldn't bear it. If Nana Jean belonged to me, she would pet my hair and I would pretend to fall asleep. I would breathe deep, smelling her homey smell, the scent of starched dresses and rising bread.

She filled his afternoon with chitchat about the weather, the meal she would make for their dinner, easy topics that poufed around them like pillows, making a warm hum that I loved so much to hear, I wished I could spy on them forever. It was clear that the one thing in this world Nana Jean most wanted to give Ziggy was the gift of everydayness. If the boy wanted to be stiff, he could be stiff. If he wanted to stay silent, he could stay silent.

"He's been through a lot lately," Nana Jean said to Lucy and Heather Anne when they came down the road with a plate of their mother's homemade Toll House cookies. Lucy held out the plate and smiled, but Ziggy's idea of a thank-you was to raise both shoulders up to his ears and growl menacingly at her, wiggling his fingers like he was casting an evil spell, and then turn away so all they could see was the back of his scruffy head and the triangular white face of the ferret peeking out from behind the mane of red hair, blinking at them in the sunlight.

Lucy stopped smiling. She made one huge sniff through her nose, smelled the ferret, and made a stink face, handing the plate to Nana Jean in a huff. She grabbed the smaller hand of Heather Anne, who stood blinking beside her, and stormed off the porch, dragging her sister behind her, to stomp back down Trowbridge Road to the Delmato house, her feathered hair so stiff with hair spray, it barely moved at all, despite all that stomping.

In the summer, six o'clock was dinnertime on Trowbridge Road. That's when the fathers started coming home from work, pulling their brown station wagons into their driveways, walking up their back steps with tired brown shoes to kiss their wives and close their doors behind them.

Six o'clock was also when mothers started calling their kids in for supper, when everyone left whatever they were doing to slump back indoors to wash their hands and faces and sit at the table when all they really wanted was to go back outside to the nicest time of any summer day, the last few hours of sunlight before bed.

At six o'clock, Nana Jean put her arm around Ziggy Karlo's skinny shoulders and walked him back inside the house with slow, easy steps. Just before he went in, Ziggy turned back around and squinted up into the copper beech tree at me. I stayed perfectly still and hid behind the curtain of leaves.

Ziggy shook his head like he was cleaning cobwebs out of his eyes and followed Nana Jean into the house. Then the screen door slammed, and I was left alone in the copper beech tree looking out on an empty neighborhood filled with closed doors and families inside their houses together, eating on plates with knives and forks and glasses clinking.

At six thirty, when everyone had already been sitting at their dinner table for half an hour, I climbed down the trunk of the copper beech tree, quiet and slow as a sloth so nobody would notice a difference when I walked the one, two, three houses down and across the street to my own sighing house with the gray shutters. The lawn needed mowing. Crabgrass reached its knotty fingers up to my kneecaps, and raspberries grew wild all along the edge.

The kids in the neighborhood thought my house was haunted. It was something about the ivy twirling up to the windows. It didn't help that most of the time, the curtains were drawn, and no one appeared to come or go from its large locked doors, not even me, June Bug Jordan, quiet as a shadow, slipping off her sandals on the sighing porch, letting herself in at six thirty-two on the dot, and then closing the door very gently behind her.

Cello Songs

The deep red notes filled the old house with echoes and made the shadows seem even darker.

I let the outside air dissolve into the familiar closed-in scent of old wood and ninety-degree days. I leaned my body against the banister that curved up the stairs, trying to wipe the last trace of the world from my skin before I entered the white room where Mother hid.

The only time that Mother ever looked connected to the earth was when she was playing her cello. She always seemed so calm when she practiced. Her hair was unfastened and loose around her shoulders. Her arms were relaxed for once, her spine straight, her two bare feet planted on the floor like the roots of a tree.

I climbed into the four-poster bed we shared and lay on my stomach with my chin in my hands to watch how the music changed her, smoothing the lines of her face, making her breathe easy and slow. Mother said that the Prelude from Bach's first suite is the most beautiful piece of music ever written for cello. It's filled with echoes, one voice singing lullabies to itself. The line glides from deep low notes to middle to high, sighing like a swan gliding over waves.

She raised her bow and let the last note shimmer in the stale air.

I sighed when it finally disappeared because the world seemed emptier without it.

Mother looked at me and smiled. She put her cello and bow down and then scuttled back to the safety of our bed.

I made room for her.

"I like that piece," I told her. "It makes me feel so peaceful."

"It always has," she said. "I used to play it when

I was pregnant with you. Used to quiet you right down. Kicking stopped. Stirring stopped. And you'd just kind of float in the darkness, listening."

She motioned for me to turn onto my side so she could hug me from behind the way she always loved to do. When I was little, I loved it too. I was the baby and she was the mommy, and we were safe together in our nest. But lately we hadn't been fitting together so well.

My stomach growled. We both heard it.

I held still and tried not to breathe.

"Mother," I said.

She didn't answer.

"Mother," I said, louder. "Is there anything to eat?"

I scrambled to my knees and looked down at her. She was still curled onto her side, holding herself now instead of me. I could see the planes of her face, the hollow of her neck, the long arms and legs jutting beneath her white nightgown.

How long had it been since she'd eaten?

My stomach growled again.

"Can you make me something?" I asked.

My voice echoed strangely in our little room.

"I don't think there's much food down there,"

said Mother. "But Uncle Toby comes with groceries on Saturday. I made him a list. Guess what's on it!"

Suddenly I was a little girl naming all the foods I loved.

"Popsicles?"

"Yup."

"And strawberries?"

"Uh-huh."

"And cheddar cheese and oranges and hot dogs and yogurt?"

"Yes, yes, yes." Mother reached up and touched the tip of my nose. "And cold cuts and yellow apples and pickles and rye bread and salami and all sorts of yummy things for my baby girl to make so she can eat all she wants."

"Like grilled cheese?"

"Of course," said Mother. "You know how to make grilled cheese. It's easy."

"But I'm hungry now."

Mother's face looked strained on the pillow. "Oh, honey," she said.

"Can't we just go down and look?"

She hesitated. Then she made herself smile. "Sure, we can go down and look," she said. "I think there might be a can of soup somewhere. I can walk down the stairs with you. But you know I don't like going into the kitchen, June. The kitchen's so close to the door. Anything can come through the cracks. And we could get very sick, June. I don't want us to get very sick."

"I know," I said. "But I don't think anything bad is going to happen."

"You can't know for sure," said Mother.

"I *do* know for sure," I said, trying to keep my voice steady and reasonable the way Daddy always used to do. "Nothing's going to come through the cracks, Mother. Nothing *ever* comes through the cracks."

"That's not true," she said. "One time it did."

I took her hand and helped her out of bed. I led her down the stairs one footstep at a time into the kitchen. She walked on tiptoes and kept her eyes on the wall, as though the faded white surface could save her somehow. I brought her to the threshold and left her clutching the carved wooden banister, halfway into the kitchen, halfway out. Then I let go of her hand and bounded into the pantry on my own.

She was right. There was one can of soup left.

I knew where the can opener was from the Chef

Boyardee Ravioli Uncle Toby had brought the week before. I found the dented saucepan under the sink even though it had a dead bee inside it. I emptied the bee onto the floor and stepped on it.

We had an antique stove, which I had to light with a wooden match. The lit gas made a blue halo around one burner. I stirred the soup with the wooden spoon and pretended that I was the mommy cooking good wholesome meals for her baby girl, and I wanted to feed her and feed her so her tummy would be full and she could grow.

See, little baby? Mommy loves you.

I stirred and hummed the kind of song I thought a cooking mommy would make.

Soon the heat from the antique stove and the heat from the summer day and the heat from the steaming soup filled the kitchen.

I poured the steaming soup from the saucepan into a bowl and then carried the bowl to the empty table, still pretending to be the mommy and the baby so happy to sit and eat together. *Mealtime. Mealtime. Come and get it.*

I sat down in the chair.

I dipped a spoon into the soup and fed myself a tiny sip.

Here you go, baby. Good for you. Yummy soup.

But then when I tasted it, I suddenly realized I couldn't get it to go down fast enough with my spoon, even when I sipped and sipped one spoonful after another.

I spooned soup so fast into baby's open mouth, she slurped and burbled. *So hungry, Mommy. So hungry I can't get full.*

I put the spoon down and picked up the bowl. There were noodles and carrot squares and tiny wonderful cubes of chicken. I raised the steaming bowl to my lips and drank and drank until soup rolled down my chin.

Queen of Fairies

One afternoon, soon after Ziggy moved in, Nana Jean brought an old calico quilt and a wicker basket onto the lawn. I perched in the tree and pretended I was sitting on the quilt along with them. We were a family. Ziggy and I were twins and Nana Jean was our mommy and we loved to be together. *Come over here, children. I have something delicious for you. There's room on the quilt for everyone.*

Ziggy's long hair was tied back in a braid. He wore a purple unicorn T-shirt. Nana Jean wore a green sleeveless sundress and a wide yellow sun hat with a curved brim that made her look like a daisy.

Watching her take the food from the picnic basket was so beautiful, it made me dizzy.

First came the basket of strawberries covered in a white cloth napkin. Then came the plate piled with more sandwiches than anyone could ever eat: egg salad and tuna salad and ham and cheese, all on white bread with the crusts cut off because that is the way we like them.

Then came the two cans of grape soda that said *pssssshhh* when we popped the tops. I pretended that Ziggy and I were drinking from the same can. He took a sip. Then I took a sip. It gave me a make-believe purple-cow mustache so sweet and so purple, I had to lick my lips and close my eyes to taste it.

Ziggy held a slice of ham out to Matthew, who sat on his haunches and snatched it with his pink hands. Then Ziggy threw another slice onto the sidewalk, and Matthew skittered away, grabbing it in his mouth and returning to his people, springing on all four feet and chattering as he went.

I was so hungry, it made my eyes water to see the ferret eating their leftovers, but then I remembered

I was pretending that I was eating too, and I held an invisible sandwich in my hands, the bread all fluffy and white, and sank my teeth in.

Egg salad. My favorite.

Nana Jean, you make the best sandwiches in the whole world.

Thank you, June Bug. I sure do love you.

I disappeared into my imagination, make-believe eating sandwiches and make-believe hugging Nana Jean and Ziggy for almost half an hour until the Crowley boys came screeching down Trowbridge Road on their bikes.

Ziggy wandered to the curb and watched them riding back and forth, playing chicken, pedaling full speed at each other and then swerving at the very last second, screeching with laughter until John-John lost control of his bike and fell off.

"Stupid fairy," said Buzz, who had a shaved head and a voice that was so ugly, it made my skin crawl.

"No, *you're* the fairy, *fairy!*" said John-John, scrambling back onto his bike and wiping the dirt off his knees.

"No, *you* are," said Buzz.

Ziggy started laughing from his place on the curb.

"What's so funny?" said Buzz.

"You," said Ziggy. "Neither of you looks even remotely like a fairy."

"Oh, and you'd know all about that, wouldn't you?" taunted Buzz.

"Actually, yes," said Ziggy. "I happen to know a great deal about fairies. For instance, most fairies have diaphanous wings. Also, they're generally much skinnier than either of you. Plus, they have large vocabularies and don't like loud noises. Or vehicles with wheels."

Buzz jerked his bike violently, and Ziggy doubled over, laughing.

"A fairy would never do that," he said.

"So, I guess that makes you king of the fairies," said Buzz.

"No," said John-John, coming closer to his brother's side and snickering. "He's the *queen,* right, Buzz? That's why he's dressed like that and he's got all that long hair like a girl."

Ziggy stopped laughing and considered this.

"Ziggy," called Nana Jean from the quilt, patting the ground beside her, "come back and finish your lunch! Bernard! Jonathan Junior! You two boys better head on home now."

John-John made a horrible face at Ziggy while Buzz looked on, smiling.

"Hey!" shouted Nana Jean. She pulled herself up from the quilt and marched to the curb with her hands on her hips.

She gave Buzz and John-John a smoldering look that could have burned a hole through rock. "Don't you dare be mean to this boy," she said. "He's been through enough. Now you turn those bikes around and ride back home before I call your mama and tell her you two rude boys are disturbing my peace. You know, I was your mama's sixth-grade teacher once upon a time, and she was scared witless of me. I can be right nasty when I mean to be, and you *do not* want me calling to complain about you. So get along home. And leave this boy alone. You hear me?"

Buzz and John-John stared at her red-faced.

"I said, do you *hear* me?"

"Yes, ma'am," muttered John-John, looking down at his feet. "We hear you."

Buzz seemed like he was going to say something hotheaded, but instead he kicked his brother in the shin, and the two boys yanked their bikes around and pedaled back down Trowbridge Road toward their house.

"I don't like those boys," said Ziggy.

"Neither do I," said Nana Jean, putting her arm around his shoulders.

"They remind me of the bullies who bothered me at school this year."

"The ones who made fun of your hair?"

"Yes," said Ziggy. "And other things."

Nana Jean took the elastic from Ziggy's braid and undid his red hair so it was long and fell past his shoulders. It looked very cheerful and bold against his purple T-shirt.

"What if I take you downtown today and we get your hair cut and maybe buy you some new clothes?" Nana Jean asked.

"I don't want new clothes," said Ziggy. "And for your information, all magical beings have long hair. If I cut my hair, I won't be able to teleport anymore."

"Is that so?" asked Nana Jean.

"Yes," said Ziggy. "It is."

Nana Jean smiled at him with her eyes so filled with love, it almost broke my heart. "Well, come on, then," she said. "Let's finish our lunch and try to forget about them. You and me, we are way too fine to let small-minded folks like that bother us."

Nana Jean led Ziggy back to the quilt and offered

him a deviled egg, which he took and liked. After that, she gave him a strawberry, and after that, a chocolate macaroon, which I could taste without even closing my eyes, and finally, when we were all full of real and imaginary things, Nana Jean put the leftovers back in the basket and Ziggy lay down with his head in her lap to look at the clouds.

Nana Jean ran her fingers through his long red hair, working at the tangles, strand by strand. Then, when it was clear she was going to need better leverage, she hoisted herself up and led him back to the porch steps, where she sat behind him.

She worked gently, coaxing out the snarls. It must have felt good to have someone's hands making your head less complicated. Nana Jean hummed while she worked, the boy wedged between her knees like a cello. She combed and hummed, taking up one frayed snarl and worrying at it until it came apart like strands of silk.

For the rest of the afternoon, they simply existed together. Nana Jean worked on her macramé owl while Ziggy and Matthew chased each other around the lawn, the boy in his purple unicorn T-shirt, throwing pinecones, the ferret leaping through the grass to find them. Sometimes Nana Jean threw back her head and laughed at something Ziggy said or did, and he grinned with crooked teeth, returning from the lawn to the porch steps every few minutes for a hug or a kiss.

I pretended I was one of them, getting kisses and hugs until five o'clock, when Ziggy began to look sleepy. Now when Nana Jean kissed him, he leaned in for longer, letting his shoulders slump, his head drooping against her. Nana Jean put her arm around him and led him slow and easy back into the house. They held the door open for Matthew, who skittered inside, thin and sleek as a wisp.

Secrets

Long after Ziggy and Nana Jean went in for dinner,
long after the fathers came home and all the other
kids disappeared into the mouths of their houses,
long after the neighborhood started to darken and
the sleepy golden evening lights turned on behind
the windows, I crept from the copper beech tree
and trudged the one, two, three houses down and
across the street to number twenty-eight. I took off
my shoes, wiped the world from my skin the best

I could, and tiptoed up the narrow staircase to our small white room.

"You're late today," Mother said from the pillows.

"I'm sorry," I said. "I lost track of time."

"What were you doing out so late?"

"Climbing trees." A half-truth.

Mother surprised me by smiling and pulling herself up. "I used to love climbing trees when I was your age," she said, delighted. She hugged the white blanket around her. "I was one of the best tree climbers in my whole school."

"You were?"

"Oh yes," she said, her eyes far away. "Oh yes. *Nothing* scared me back then. I would climb up and look out at the world. You can see *so* many things from the top of a tree. So many *beautiful* things."

"I know," I said, smiling at her excitement. "I like that too. Maybe next time you could come out with me. I bet you could still climb trees if you tried."

"No," said Mother. "I couldn't." She slumped back down on to the mattress and curled toward the pillows again.

I wanted her to be better so badly, it was worse than being hungry. I started to climb toward her into our bed, but Mother took a deep breath through her nose and her face contorted into a horrible mask.

"Wait," she said, her voice catching in her throat.

"What?"

"Go wash up first. Your hands and your face, especially. You smell a little."

"I do?"

"Yes," said Mother. "You definitely smell. Use soap and hot water. Then you can come back, and we can read our books together until it's time to go to bed. Please, June Bug. Wash. And then come back to me. That's my sweet girl."

I did as I was told. Even though it was barely eight o'clock and I knew I wouldn't be able to get to sleep for hours, especially on an empty stomach.

I filled the sink with hot water and used the soap to scrub my hands and face, rubbing back and forth across my lips until I was fresh and clean.

Then I found my book and climbed back into bed.

I lifted the covers and lay down beside her, turning toward the wall. I opened the book and pretended to read, but the lines were all blurry on account of my tears.

"I missed you today," I said to the wall.

"I missed you too, sweetheart," said Mother, her voice far away. "I always miss you waiting here all alone."

But I knew I was not the one she really missed.

The Patchwork Prince

Most nights Daddy would come home late, long after Ryles Jazz Club was closed and the last outbound Green Line train from Boston pulled into Newton Highlands station.

He would walk through town in the dark and into our sleeping house, still dressed in his favorite patchwork coat and his faded linen shirt. He would put his satchel by the door, pour himself a glass of wine, and fall asleep at the kitchen table, where we would often find him in the morning, with his cloth fedora still tipped over his eyes.

He was tall and willowy like a dancer. Soft-spoken. His eyes were deep and gray and he had such long eyelashes that whenever I looked at him, I was moved to take his hands into my own and stroke them.

When I was small enough to fit in his lap, I would cuddle up and scratch my fingers into his beard and kiss his chin until my lips tickled. This was before the virus left him a pale shadow lying in the hospital bed we set up for him in the dining room so he wouldn't have to climb the stairs.

The dining room was the first place to fill with morning light, and it had a high ceiling so he wouldn't feel quite so closed in. Mother hired men to carry out the dining room table and move in the grand piano so he could spend the day playing music. When he was tired, he could lie down in the hospital bed. When he needed a bathroom, he could stagger across the hall.

When we knew the end was really coming, Mother began closing off the rooms of our house. She told me it was because it was easier this way, to keep things clean, and with AIDS, clean meant safe. Daddy was allowed to be sick in the dining room and bathroom. I was allowed to be well in the kitchen and upstairs in my parents' bedroom. The other rooms, the places we used to pass through every day of our lives—his study, Mother's music studio, my old bedroom, the living room, the guest bedrooms—these were all off-limits because it was too hard to know where the germs were hiding.

That's when Mother first brought me into her bed at night, to make sure I was sleeping in a clean place. Eventually, she moved me in full-time and began calling it "our room," meaning that it belonged to her and me, rather than her and Daddy.

Nobody knew very much about the disease. We didn't know if it could be left on doorknobs or toilet seats. We didn't know if you could get it if an infected person coughed or breathed on you. We didn't know if it traveled through tears, or if you could catch it through a kiss. So when Daddy started dying, the dining room and the downstairs bathroom were also off-limits to me. I would sit in the hallway or at the kitchen table and call out to him, *Daddy, Daddy,* and if he was awake, he would call back to me, *June Bug, June Bug,* which is how I knew he was still okay.

Even in his last weeks, Daddy's music filled our house, played with shaking hands amidst jags of coughing, but music nonetheless. Sometimes Mother would bring her cello into the dining room and play with him, making her instrument wail like the velvet voice of Ella Fitzgerald, scatting around his melody, the sweet, mournful riffs of a soul getting ready to say goodbye.

Even though she kept me from touching him, and even though she always made sure to scrub her hands with bleach and hot water after tending to him, Mother never left Daddy alone for too long. She would move between him and me, reading me poetry in the kitchen with a glass of milk and a grilled cheese sandwich, but then, when he called out, pulling on a pair of disposable latex gloves to hold his hand while he wept. Our trash bins filled with latex gloves, translucent and dry as snake skins.

She had all kinds of ways to keep me occupied. Sketchbooks. Modeling clay. Watercolors. When she went to him for too long, I would call for her, making sure my voice was loud enough for both of them to hear me. There was always something I needed. A book I couldn't reach. A meal I couldn't make.

"Mother!" I called out on the last day of his life, my voice so shrill, I knew it would make her jump to attention. "Mother! Aren't you going to make me something for lunch?"

Her tired voice came from the dining room. "Just a minute, June. Daddy needs me."

"I need you!" I called back. "I'm *hungry!*"

"Oh, for goodness' sake, June. You are ten years old. Just make something *yourself* for once."

I punished her when she returned, shrinking away when she reached toward me.

She went to the counter, and I could hear her making my lunch. She brought back a glass of milk and a bologna and Wonder Bread sandwich.

When she offered me the plate, I pushed it out of her hands, and it crashed to the floor. There was a puddle of milk and sandwich fixings everywhere, but the plate didn't break; it just clattered and spun. I remember how disappointed I was, because a broken plate would have been much more dramatic. I started to cry.

"Honey," said Mother, "please try to understand. I'm doing the best I can. I really am."

"No, you're not," I said. "I told you I was hungry and you didn't care."

"I did care." Mother sighed. She started to clean up the mess. "I *do* care, sweetheart. But Daddy needed me just then. You can make your own lunch. Daddy can't clean himself up. Can you try to understand that? He needs me more than you do right now."

"Daddy always needs you!" I screamed in her face.

"God help me, June. Your father is dying. Pretty soon we won't have him anymore. You've got your whole life to spend with me."

"Why doesn't he hurry up and die then!" I screeched. "Why don't you hurry up and die, Daddy! Hurry up and die right this second for all I care!"

Mother slapped me.

I held myself, stunned by the force of our anger.

Mother knelt on the floor beside me.

"I'm sorry, Mother," I whispered, reaching out to her.

She leaned her head against the wall and sobbed.

"I didn't mean what I said. I don't want Daddy to die."

She lifted her head to look at me. Her eyes were filled with shadows.

"I know that, honey," she said, softly. "We're

both tired—we don't know what we're saying or doing anymore. You didn't mean to hurt me."

"I did mean to hurt you," I said. "But I'm sorry."

Mother kissed me on the forehead. Her lips were warm. "I forgive you," she said.

"I want to tell Daddy I'm sorry too. He might have heard what I said."

"You can't go in his room, sweetheart. You know that."

"I'll stand in the hall. I'll tell him from there."

"Okay," Mother said. "I'll come with you."

She took me by the hand, and we walked from the kitchen into the hallway.

Daddy was lying in his hospital bed in the dining room, facing us.

His eyes were open and he was smiling like he had been waiting for us to come.

"I'm sorry, Daddy," I said. "I didn't mean what I said."

But it was too late. He was gone.

Morning Glory

On Saturdays, Uncle Toby arrived early because he knew I'd be hungry.

During this past school year, he came all the way to Newton even though he had to drive in from his basement apartment in Somerville every morning to give me breakfast and bring me to school before heading back out to the lumberyard. He always had a ham and egg sandwich or a couple of cold pancakes or, if I was really lucky, maybe a packet of Hostess Twinkies. After school, he always had something for me from the pizza place: a slice of pepperoni, a wedge of baklava, half an Italian sub. I never asked him how it felt having to drive back and forth every day. But I was grateful.

Now that school was out for the summer, Mother said we only needed him once a week with groceries. Uncle Toby said he'd rather keep coming twice a day just like he'd been doing, but Mother said, "No thank you, we'll be just fine. You don't need to be driving so much, day after day. Doesn't the lumberyard pay by the hour? You need to work, Toby. And besides, it's time for me and June Bug to try and make it on our own now."

As soon as we heard Uncle Toby's truck rattle into our driveway, my own mother, Angela Jordan, who once played Bach suites to a packed audience of sneezing strangers without even batting an eyelash, now pulled the blanket over her head and stewed in her own sweat.

According to Mother, body odor was okay because it came from the inside. It was the germs from the outside that could kill us: surfaces that were touched or sneezed on by strangers. It was the toilet seats and doorknobs and hands and mouths of strangers that could devour us and spit out our bones.

I knew that to Mother, Uncle Toby was still a stranger even though he was Daddy's younger brother, and even though he was born right here in this very house, and even though he said he loved us so much, it made him want to get down on his knees and pray, which was really something because Uncle Toby did not believe in God.

I careened down the stairs, whooping like a crazy bird to meet my favorite man alive, two steps at a time, vaulting over the carved banister, leaving the scent of Mother's skin behind me like a fading dream.

"June Bug!" Uncle Toby called from the kitchen in a voice that sounded like Thanksgiving. "Where's my little mongoose? Hope she didn't chew off her own tail."

All at once, the house was filled with the wondrous sound of paper grocery bags, of footsteps from the door to the long, empty table, of leather work boots clomping dirt and germs and forbidden outside-things onto the floor of the kitchen, filling me with a happiness that spread through my veins like helium, making me feel like I could lift to the ceiling and fly.

"June Bug? Where are you?" he called out,

pretending to search for me even when I stopped an inch away from him. I stepped on both his boots with my bare feet, and he waltzed me around the kitchen like a marionette.

When the dancing stopped, I watched him put the food away, each item emerging from the grocery bag like a rabbit from a magician's hat, food I would prepare myself that week without Mother's help: cold cuts and chocolate pudding, cheddar cheese and Popsicles, hot dogs and cans of chicken soup, yogurt and macaroni, peanut butter and Wonder Bread, purple grape juice (the kind that made your lips pucker), strawberries, and grapes and chocolate chip cookies.

He made me a snack plate so I wouldn't be too hungry watching him put the food away — a sampler of different treats: a cookie, a hunk of cheese, a bunch of grapes, three slices of roast beef, a piece of white bread smeared with peanut butter.

I wolfed it down.

Uncle Toby sat next to me and rubbed my back while I ate, petting my shoulders and pushing my hair back behind my ears.

"Easy there," he said. "Not all at once. Give it a chance to go down."

Mother's thin voice came from the blankets upstairs. "Hi, Toby," she called. "You almost finished down there? You've been here a long time, and I think you'd better get going now. We don't want to keep you. Thank you for coming. See you next week."

"Hold your horses," Uncle Toby called up the stairs. "Why don't you come down and join us, Angela? Or I could bring something up to you if you want. You eating anything these days, or are you living on air and eighth notes?"

We heard Mother's voice try to laugh. She would have lived on air and eighth notes if it had been possible, but as it was, she had to have actual food every now and then. Just enough to keep her alive.

Uncle Toby picked up my wrist between two fingers and frowned. "You're looking like you could use a little meat on your bones too, June Bug," Uncle Toby told me quietly so Mother couldn't hear. "Your daddy would be mad at me if he knew I was letting you get skinny. Maybe I should start coming over more often. Would you like that? Bet you get lonely sometimes now that school's out."

There was no way on earth he could know the truth of his words. There was no way he could know how incomplete the word *lonely* could be when it stood back-to-back with loneliness, or how hungry a girl could get for so much more than food.

"You know, I miss spending time in this big old house. Your daddy and I had lots of fun running around this kitchen, making your poor grandma crazy. How about if I start coming twice a week?"

"I would like that," I told him simply, because I had no words for the rest of what was true.

"Angie?" called Uncle Toby up the stairs. "Next time, I'm coming up there with a sandwich. What kind do you like? Salami? Liverwurst?"

There was no answer.

"You better go," I told him. "We'll be fine."

"You sure?" Uncle Toby put his hands on either side of my face and looked into my eyes, which everyone said were so much like Daddy's. "What are you doing with yourself during the day now that school's out? You staying in this house all the time with your mom?"

"No," I said, smiling. "I have a new friend."

"A friend?"

Suddenly, a story about Ziggy Karlo and Nana Jean came pouring out of my mouth, so sweet to say, so sweet to hear, that I almost believed the lies as soon as the first syllables passed through my lips. The lies were almost like a wish, and as soon as I began, I knew I'd have to make it come true.

"We play all the time," I said, feeling my eyes widen. "And I eat lunch and dinner at his house most days. His nana makes us food. Anything we want. Lasagna. Ravioli. She's such a good cook, Uncle Toby. And she's really nice. She helps take care of me. And sometimes, when Mother isn't feeling good, I sleep in their spare room, and she tucks me in and kisses me good night, and she checks on me three times during the night to make sure I'm okay."

Uncle Toby wrapped his arms around me. "Oh, June Bug," he said, sighing. "That's wonderful news. Nana Jean is exactly what you need right now."

I hugged him and he pulled me close so I could feel his beard scratch my cheeks.

"You don't have to worry, Uncle Toby," I said, still warm from my wish. "Everything is going to be okay."

Rules for Staying Clean

Mother waited until she could hear Uncle Toby's truck pull out of our driveway to finally make her way downstairs in her white cotton nightgown, her hair plastered to her face, one hand holding the railing, and the other holding the neck of her nightgown closed.

"Are you going to take a shower?" I asked her.

"After we get this place cleaned up," she said.

Usually, disinfection took about two and a half hours, but that was on a normal day when no one brought anything new into the house. On Saturdays, when Uncle Toby came, the time could be doubled or tripled.

There were thousands of possible points of disgustingness on the paper bags and grocery items themselves, which had been handled by strangers — farmworkers, factory workers, movers, packagers, grocery-store stock boys and check-out clerks — and all these people had shaken hands with someone, or wiped themselves without washing, or sneezed into their hands. Even Uncle Toby, who put the food away into our refrigerator and cupboards, could have tracked anything from the world into the kitchen on his hands or the soles of his boots.

For all these reasons, Saturday disinfection could sometimes take all day.

Each step caught the germs left over from the last. There were rules we had to follow no matter what.

Here are some examples of the rules:

Always start from the highest places and work your way down.

Germs from the second floor can fall down the stairs onto the first.

Germs from the walls can fall to the counters, can fall

to the floor, can get trapped beneath your feet and then spread back into the rest of the house, so you always do the first floor last with a brand-new bucket of bleach.

It's important to protect your hands whenever possible, because hands accidentally touch eyes and mouth and all the other inside places and then the germs attack the body and you die.

Mother kept crates of surgical gloves in the pantry and went through five or six boxes during a usual Saturday disinfection.

According to Mother, you could only safely use a pair of surgical gloves for the disinfection of a single large item or three smaller items.

Here are some examples of large items: a wall, a table, a countertop.

Here are some examples of small items: a toaster, a faucet, a telephone.

This rule meant that Mother needed to change gloves ten or fifteen times per room.

The main problem with the surgical gloves was that in order to take them off your hands, you had to use your fingers, which meant coming into contact with the disgustingness.

Surgeons, of course, know how to do this without touching anything contaminated.

First, they rinse their gloves in antiseptic—in our case, Clorox bleach—then they remove one glove halfway, and the other halfway, then they take the fingertips of one glove to put the other glove in the garbage and then their bare fingers to remove the remaining glove, being careful, of course, to only touch the inside-out part, as not to contaminate the skin.

The problem with Mother's method was this: she never trusted the inside-out part. What if there was disgustingness under the glove? What if it somehow seeped through the microscopic fissures of the latex, or under the fingernail, where it might fester, nibbling at the cuticles and eventually destroying the entire finger, gnawing at the hand until it looked like hamburger?

This meant that she would sometimes get stuck in a never-ending loop of putting on and taking off surgical gloves until she was satisfied that she had done it perfectly.

Most of the time, I helped her disinfect. After all, if it hadn't been for my need to eat so much, Uncle Toby wouldn't have had to bring food so often, and the process of cleaning would have been much simpler. I went along with the rules and scrubbed obediently, helping her move from top to bottom as quickly as I could.

But today, my story about Ziggy Karlo and Nana Jean ate at me, and I found myself sitting on the kitchen stairs, watching Mother tornado from one object to the next, her face pinched and white, and all I wanted was to make the story real.

I wanted Ziggy Karlo to be my friend. I wanted the ferret to dance at my feet. I wanted Nana Jean to tell the neighbor kids that I had been through a hard time so it was okay for me to be unfriendly. There would be good things cooking inside, and there would be calming talk about nothing at all, and a shoulder to lean against, and old lady skin that smelled like talcum powder and rose perfume.

"Mother," I said.

She scrubbed the counter with a bristle brush, back and forth, back and forth, her breath coming out in jagged gasps.

"Mother," I said again. "I'm going out to climb trees."

She continued scrubbing. "I can't get this off," she said.

"I'll be back at my regular time. Six thirty-two on the dot."

"I keep trying, but I just can't do it." She pushed harder and moved faster, and the kitchen was filled with the furious sound of bristles scratching the wood.

"Okay," I said. "Bye, Mother."

She didn't look up from her scrubbing. The whole room warmed from her movement, churning into a strange mixture of bleach and sweat, the two scents so strong, I forced myself to inhale and exhale through my mouth all the way from the kitchen, down the hall to the parlor, and out the door.

Outside, I leaned against the porch rail and breathed the wonderful outdoor air filled with the green smell of leaves and grass and sun and cars and people, a feast of fresh air cascading into my screaming, delirious lungs.

Transformation

When I got to the copper beech tree, Ziggy Karlo was waiting for me cross-legged on the longest branch. He was wearing an orange Dungeons & Dragons T-shirt and green corduroys with red bandanna patches on the knees. Matthew the ferret was curled on top of his head like a strange white cap.

"Hey," said Ziggy.

"Hey," I said. "How's it going?"

"Pretty good," said Ziggy. "Except for the fact that there's this nosy neighbor girl who keeps spying on me. She climbs up this tree right here, and she watches everything I do."

"I'm sorry," I said, feeling my cheeks redden.

"Did you think I wouldn't notice?"

"I guess not," I said. "I guess I didn't think you could see me."

"Well, I *did* see you," said Ziggy. "I saw you every time. Looking down at me. Staring like I was some kind of freak. And I didn't appreciate it."

"I'm sorry," I said. "I didn't mean to make you feel weird."

"You didn't *make* me feel weird," said Ziggy. "I don't need to be *made* to feel weird. I *am* weird. I am an entirely different kind of creature from most people around here. And for your information, I'm *used* to people staring at me. Everyone at my old school stared at me. The kids in *this* neighborhood stare at me. And now you stare at me too."

"I wasn't staring at you," I said, suddenly breathless because of how hard my heart was beating.

Ziggy narrowed his eyes at my lie.

"Well," I amended, "I mean, I guess I *was* staring at you. But not in the way you think. I didn't mean to make you feel bad. It's just that I like watching people. I like how your nana talks to you. I like how

53

she hugs you and makes you things to eat and takes the snarls out of your hair. It's beautiful."

"You think my nana is beautiful?" asked Ziggy, looking at me sideways.

I nodded.

"I think she's beautiful too," he admitted. "She has always been an exquisite matriarch."

"You use interesting words," I told him.

"I do?"

"Yes," I said. "Just now, you used the words *exquisite matriarch*. That's beautiful. You have a good vocabulary. You told Buzz and John-John that fairies have *diaphanous* wings, and I have never heard a person use the word *diaphanous* before. It's an unusual word. I like it."

"I like it too," said Ziggy.

We were both silent for a few moments, just watching each other and wondering.

"Anyway," I said, sighing, "I'm sorry I made you feel like I was staring at you. I'll go home now if you want me to. I won't bother you anymore."

I took a deep breath and turned to go. Trowbridge Road stretched in front of me with its row of tall Victorian houses, each with its own closed door. I started walking.

"Wait a second," said Ziggy suddenly.

I whirled around. "What?"

"I was just thinking. If you would be willing to sit *with* me in this tree, I feel like perhaps I would rather *enjoy* it."

"Do you mean that?"

"I never say anything I don't mean," said Ziggy. "That's one of the many peculiar things about me that most people don't like. It's unfortunate. Anyway, I think this branch is big enough for two people to sit together, don't you?"

"Yes," I said, feeling myself blush with the happiness of a wish coming true. "I think we'd fit just fine."

"Do you want a hand?" He leaned down from the branch and offered me one.

"No thank you," I said. "I've been up this tree so many times, I could climb it with my eyes closed."

"Show me," said Ziggy.

I closed my eyes and reached up the trunk with the palms of my hands until I found the first burl. I pulled myself up and found my foothold and then reached up for the next one, and the next one. I pulled myself up on a branch and put one leg over, then leaned on my belly and made my way around to the thickest branch, where there was a wide notch exactly the right size for my body. I leaned against the trunk, opened my eyes, and sighed.

"Voilà," I said.

Ziggy looked over at me and smiled. His teeth were crooked. The summer sun shone through the leaves and made his long red hair even more brilliant. Nana Jean sat on the wicker chair. She rocked back and forth the way a woman might do if she had a baby in her arms. She took a pin out of her bun and let the silver hair fall loose around her shoulders. Then she leaned her head against the back of the rocking chair and closed her eyes. The breeze blew her hair below and the leaves above.

"It's so peaceful up here," I said.

"It is," agreed Ziggy. "But it's nothing compared to the ninth dimension."

"What's the ninth dimension?"

"It's a place you can only go if you are magical," said Ziggy.

"Magical?"

"Like you and me."

"I don't know any magic."

"Yes, you do. I can tell by the way you climbed up with your eyes closed. You're not like other kids.

You are like me. A nomad. Born to wander to the ninth dimension and then back to earth. But first we have to cast a spell on each other."

"What kind of spell?"

"An inspiration spell. Inspiration means to breathe, and before we wander we have to weave our inspiration together so we don't get separated. I will blow my air at you and you will inhale, and then you will blow your air at me and I will inhale, and this way our breath will be woven together and we will be ready to travel."

Mother didn't like the idea of accidentally inhaling other people's air. Our own breath passes over our lips, which is close to the tongue and the inside of the mouth, a sure path to disgustingness. The mouth was off-limits. If I ever stuck my finger in there, bit off a hangnail, picked a piece of carrot from between my teeth, or, worse than that, if my thumb found my mouth, an old habit, Mother would tell me to disinfect with bleach. But now there was no bleach around. Mother was far away. All there was in the whole world was this copper beech tree and the ferret and this strange red-haired boy.

"In order for the spell to work correctly, we both have to inhale and exhale as deeply as possible.

Here . . ." He took a strip of Wrigley's Spearmint gum out of his shirt pocket, unwrapped it, broke it, and gave one half to me. "We should chew this until our breath feels minty. Minty breath is colder, and it will make the magic run faster."

This sounded logical.

I took my half and chewed.

Ziggy chewed too.

Soon, the air around us smelled not only like ferret and bark and leaves, but like spearmint, and all we could hear was the sound of our chewing, and the ferret chattering from the top of Ziggy's head, and then the birds chirping, and Nana Jean humming with her eyes closed, with the quiet backdrop of the neighborhood swirling around us.

We swung our feet back and forth and watched Nana Jean put one hand through her hair and across her forehead.

"Maybe we should wait until she goes inside," I suggested. "Just in case she looks up or something."

"Okay," said Ziggy. "Nana Jean usually has to go in every hour or so. She says she can't hold it like she used to. She wears special old lady diapers called Depends. This is what you call *apropos,* which is a

Greek word meaning appropriate. Now here is a non sequitur, which means I am changing the subject. When you inspire me, you have to imagine the whole universe coming out of your mouth like a spiderweb shooting right into my mouth. Can you do that?"

"I don't know," I told him, after a long pause. "I've never imagined the universe coming out of my mouth like a spiderweb. I'm not even sure I can picture that. I guess I'm just going to have to give it a try and find out."

"Yes," said Ziggy. "I guess you will just have to try. I'm glad you're imaginative and brave. Imagination and bravery are very good qualities to have in the ninth dimension. It helps with things like dragons and other mystical beasts."

"I've never been afraid of dragons," I said.

The ferret climbed from Ziggy Karlo's head to his shoulder, and from his shoulder through his T-shirt and onto his lap.

"He's cute," I said. "How long have you had him?"

"Jenny gave him to me as a birthday present when I turned eight, and he has never left my side since then. His name is Matthew. He is an albino ferret. He's also my vestigial twin. You can pet him if you want."

I held out one hand, and the long white creature sniffed at me. Then he grabbed my finger with his claw and took a bite.

"Hey," I said. "Stop it."

I started to pull my finger away, but the ferret hung on tight. I scratched him behind his velvety ears, and he put his chin on Ziggy's knee and closed his eyes like a puppy.

"He likes you," Ziggy said.

"All animals like me."

"That will be good for wandering in the ninth dimension. I didn't tell you this, but I am part animal."

"I'm part animal too," I said.

"I *knew* it," said Ziggy. "That's why you're so good at climbing trees. You're probably part squirrel. Or possibly crow."

"Maybe both," I suggested.

"Maybe," agreed Ziggy. He raised one eyebrow and looked at me thoughtfully.

Ziggy placed Matthew farther out on the branch. The creature circled a few times, curled up, and put his white tail over his nose. I petted him quietly for a while, and then I smelled my hand. It was musky. Not quite as strong as skunk but wild and sharp. Mother wouldn't like it. I wiped my hand on my knees.

Nana Jean lifted her head from the back of the rocking chair, smoothed out her skirt, and rose to her feet.

"Look," I said, happily. "Your nana is going inside to pee."

"Huzzah," said Ziggy. "Are you ready to do the inspiration spell?"

"I was born ready."

It took some maneuvering, but I knew how to keep my balance. I swung one leg over the branch so that I was facing him. Then I put my two hands in front of me and opened my mouth.

Ziggy took a deep breath and leaned forward, just a little, just so he could get better aim. He closed his eyes, like he was gathering the universe inside himself, and then he blew a whooshing arrow of minty, ferrety air straight at me. I inhaled quickly, imagining the universe swirling into my lungs.

"Did you get any?"

"I think so," I said.

"That's good," said Ziggy. "Now you inspire me."

I took a deep breath, leaned forward, and blew as hard as I could toward Ziggy's face. I imagined stars spiraling from my mouth and swirling into Ziggy. I imagined mothers and fathers and grandparents and all the people who had ever been born diving through the air in a silvery cloud of spirits.

Ziggy swallowed and swayed a little, his eyes fluttering.

"That was very good," he said.

"Thank you," I said. "So what should we do next?"

"I guess I should ask your name," said Ziggy. "If you and I are going to wander the universe together, I should know what to call you in case one of us gets lost."

"People call me June Bug," I told him. "But my real name is June Jordan."

"June Bug is better," he said. "It's more unusual, which is better for a nomad. Why did they name you June Bug? Were you born in June?"

"No," I said. "I was born in February."

"I was born in October, which is the rainy season in the ninth dimension. No one even knows about the ninth dimension but Jenny and you. And Matthew of course, because he's a ferret and all ferrets are clairvoyant. You should probably know that I have the ability to move objects with my mind. This is not unusual for nomads of the ninth dimension, but it is unusual in the world of mortals. The paranormal term for this talent is *telekinesis.* That's a good five-syllable word. You could get a lot of Scrabble points if you knew how to spell it, especially if you got a triple-word score. One time when I was six months old, Jenny was having a party and when she came into the kitchen, I had three open Budweiser cans spinning above my crib. Like a mobile. It was cool. I can still do that."

"Just with beer cans?"

Ziggy laughed. "I like you," he said. "You're funny."

"Everyone in school says I'm too serious."

"They must not know you very well," said Ziggy.

"They don't."

"People at my school don't know me very well, either," Ziggy said.

"Why?" I asked him.

"I don't know," said Ziggy. "Probably because I barely ever go."

"Are you sick a lot?"

"No," said Ziggy. "Jenny and I just can't deal sometimes."

"Oh," I said.

I looked over at him. His eyes were far away so I didn't tell him about the winter mornings when I had to get myself ready for school while Mother lay in bed, the blankets pulled up to her chin, how I rose in the darkness to clean and dress myself, to gather my things for school, and then tiptoed downstairs to wait at the empty kitchen table for Uncle Toby to arrive with breakfast.

I didn't tell him how in the mornings I watched the clock drip from one minute to the next like melted wax falling from a candle—6:30, 6:45, 6:50—until I finally heard the keys in the back door and then Uncle Toby was there, stomping the snow off his work boots and pulling my breakfast out of a paper bag. Sometimes he would reach over to rub my back or push a stray lock of hair behind my ear. I always liked that, because his hands, although they were hard and calloused, looked a lot like Daddy's. When I was full, I would put down my fork and curl my hand inside his.

I put my hand on the branch near Ziggy's hand.

"You look like you want something," Ziggy said.

"I do want something, but it feels funny to ask."

"You can ask me anything," said Ziggy. "I won't do it if I don't want to."

"Are you sure?"

"Yes," said Ziggy. "I am sure."

"Will you hold my hand? For just a second?"

"You want me to hold your hand?"

I thought about Uncle Toby's hands and Daddy's hands, and I thought about how my own hand felt nestled inside theirs, warm and safe like an egg.

"Yes," I said. "If you don't mind."

Ziggy thought about it.

"I don't mind," he said.

I put out my hand.

Ziggy took it carefully.

His fingernails were ragged, chewed almost to the quick.

We sat side by side on the branch looking at our hands and not saying anything.

Trowbridge Road stretched beneath our feet.

Someone was playing an old Beatles record. We could hear it, smoky and fragile, rising up to the branches.

There were other things we could only hear

properly with our eyes closed. A baseball hitting a glove. The sound of Mr. Moniker's crazy old dog barking at squirrels. And then farther down the road, the sounds of neighborhood kids laughing. I heard them before I could see them coming. Heather Anne was riding on the handlebars of Lucy's pink banana-seat bike, and Buzz and John-John Crowley were swerving back and forth, trying to crash into them.

"You stop that, Buzz Crowley," scolded Lucy when Heather Anne almost went flying.

They hollered all the way to Nana Jean's house, where they circled around like two-wheeled vultures.

"Where is he?" asked John-John.

"He's inside," Buzz said.

"What do you think he's *doing* in there?" asked Heather Anne from her place on the handlebars.

"Probably playing with his stinky rat," said Lucy.

Ziggy stiffened at the word *rat*.

"Probably flouncing around like a fairy," said Buzz, standing up on his pedals to get a better look at the house.

Buzz laughed. John-John looked over at his brother, and then he laughed too.

Ziggy looked at me. His eyes were sad and scared.

"Did you see his hair?" asked John-John. "Did you see how long his hair is?"

"Yeah, we saw it," said Lucy.

"And we *smelled* it too," crowed Heather Anne.

Everyone laughed until the screen door slammed and Nana Jean marched onto the porch and down the steps to tower on the sidewalk with her hands on her hips. She glared at all four children until they turned their bikes around and pedaled as hard as they could down the street, Lucy with Heather Anne on the handlebars and Buzz and John-John on their own bikes, riding away as fast as they could.

Nana Jean stayed on the sidewalk until they were out of sight. Then she sighed, wiped the palms of her hands across her dress, and rolled her silver hair back into a bun.

"Ziggy?" she called out into the neighborhood. "Lunchtime, Ziggy. Come on back inside now."

Ziggy's face was red. "Did you hear them?" he asked, his voice wavering. "Did you hear what they said about me?"

"Yes," I said. "I heard what they said about you."

Ziggy tried to drag one hand through his hair,

but he couldn't quite do it because of the snarls. He smelled his fingers and then dropped his hand down into his lap.

"Do you think my hair smells bad?" he asked. His eyes were wide.

I leaned over and breathed in though my nose. He smelled like ferret.

"No," I said. "I like the way your hair smells."

"Are you sure?"

"Yes," I said. "I'm sure."

"Good," said Ziggy. "The boys at my school were always saying mean things. And I never knew if they were true or not."

"Ziggy!" called Nana Jean again.

"I need to go," said Ziggy, his face still red like he had been slapped. "If you come back tomorrow, I can show you how to use the psychic powers granted to you by birth as a nomad of the ninth dimension."

"I would like that very much," I said.

Ziggy put Matthew back on top of his head.

"Remember, June Bug," he said. "There is always more to this world than what you can see with your eyes."

"I believe you," I said.

Ziggy smiled his crooked smile.

"Ziggy!" called Nana Jean again.

"I've got to go now."

"I'll see you tomorrow."

"I'll be right here waiting for you," said Ziggy.

Ziggy waved his hands with a flourish, weaving invisible patterns into the air. Then he grinned, swung to a lower branch, and made his way down.

The copper leaves rustled as he descended until he was standing on firm ground. Then he made his way across the lawn and back onto the porch. Nana Jean put her arm around him, kissed his cheek, and walked him inside, where there was a bowl of hot cheese ravioli waiting for him. I could smell it, the delicious steam rising from the open windows of Nana Jean's kitchen, salty and warm as a miracle.

Dandelion Silk

The next day, Ziggy was waiting for me in the copper beech tree just like he promised he would. When I squinted into the silvery branches, I could see his feet in their battered green sneakers and his bare legs dangling over the branch. I could see orange gym shorts and a flower-power T-shirt with a faded yellow peace sign in the middle. His wild hair was pulled into a messy ponytail that hung down over the same shoulder where Matthew was perched, batting absently at the loose strands and then above at the copper beech leaves with his tiny pink hands.

"Salutations," said Ziggy when he saw me.

"Hey," I said. "I worried you weren't going to be here."

"Where else would I be?" said Ziggy.

"I don't know," I said, smiling. "Maybe hanging out with those Crowley boys?"

"You're funny," said Ziggy. "Come up. I brought you something."

"What is it?" I asked.

"Lunch."

I scrambled up as fast I could, swinging my leg onto the longest branch and then pulling myself up beside him. I was out of breath when Ziggy handed over the jar of cheese ravioli. "Nana Jean made this for me yesterday," he said. "I thought you'd like it. We'll need extra sustenance for our travels today. Cheese ravioli is perfect for wandering. Go ahead. It's good. I promise."

I unscrewed the lid and salty tendrils of cheese and tomatoes swirled from the jar.

"Go on," said Ziggy again. "It's okay."

I took one ravioli from the jar by its corner and tasted it. It was heavenly. Then I took another. Then, before I knew it, I was shoving one ravioli after another into my mouth with my fingers while

Ziggy leaned against the trunk watching. I licked the tomato sauce from my fingers as though I were drinking milk from a bottle.

"You were hungry," said Ziggy.

I nodded, running my tongue along the inside of the jar to get the last drops.

Ziggy reached over for the empty jar and hung it on the stump of a broken branch.

"In the ninth dimension, no one is ever hungry," he said. "You can get full just by breathing."

"That sounds perfect."

"It is," said Ziggy.

"And no one in the ninth dimension is ever cruel. And no one is ever alone. And everyone is brave. And you can make anything you want happen, just by wishing. Do you remember the word I taught you yesterday that means moving objects with your mind?"

"Telekinesis," I said.

"Right," said Ziggy. "Every nomad of the ninth dimension knows how to use it. For most of us, it's as natural as breathing. We can simply look at any object, reach out with our mind, tell the object to move, *and the object will move.*"

My heart was pounding. "I want to do that," I said.

"We have to cast the inspiration spell on each other one more time. Just to make sure we are woven together. Are you ready?"

"I was born ready, remember?" I said.

Ziggy blew hard. I closed my eyes and inhaled. I could taste the Victorian houses and the green lawns and the suntan lotion. I could taste the greatest hits of 1983 coming from someone's boom box far away, and Nana Jean's macramé owls and the ravioli. Then I blew my air back at him, a spiraling spiderweb.

"How do you feel?" asked Ziggy.

"Tingly," I told him.

"Me too," said Ziggy. "That's how you know the magic's working. Now look up."

I could see the silvery branches of the copper beech reaching above us, the beautiful red leaves making a canopy between earth and the blue beyond.

"See all those leaves?" Ziggy asked.

"Of course, I see them."

"There's no breeze, right?"

"Right. No breeze."

"Okay. Watch what I do. I'm going to look into the leaves and concentrate until I can feel them with the tips of my fingers. Then I'm going to extend my mind and make them move."

Ziggy raised his face to the sky. He seemed to grow taller. He moved his wrists and hands and his fingers all around him, as though the leaves far above his head were close enough to touch.

At first nothing happened. But then a breeze came through and the leaves started flickering. They quaked and crackled above us.

I shrieked with joy. "You did it!"

Matthew jumped up on his tiptoes and bounced back to Ziggy's shoulder.

"Yes," said Ziggy. "And now *you're* going to do it."

I stared at the leaves.

Nothing happened.

"I can't," I said.

"You can," said Ziggy. "You're a nomad. You understand the language of the trees. Look up at the leaves. Extend your mind. And they will move!"

I stared at the branches and leaves above me. I tried to send my mind to where the branches curled and crisscrossed.

I clenched my teeth and pushed, but I didn't feel anything special.

"You're trying too hard," said Ziggy. "Take a deep breath and send yourself up there."

"I *can't*," I said again.

"You can," said Ziggy. "I'm with you. Can you feel me? I'm bringing you up into the branches. I'm lifting you."

At first, I didn't feel anything, but then I could feel him, below me, lifting me like I was a dancer. "It's like wind," I said. "Like I'm rising on a big pillow of air."

"That's it!" said Ziggy. "That's how it's supposed to feel. Now you do the rest by yourself. Lift yourself up until your face is right underneath the leaves. Until it tickles your cheeks."

My face was tilted toward the sky and I was rising into the branches. I could feel the copper canopy touching my cheeks and my forehead.

"Now reach out with your hands and touch the leaves. Make them move."

I bent my wrists and hands and fingers the way Ziggy did, wandering them through the air, flickering them around me like wind. The leaves began to wave along with my fingers, first just one leaf, then another and another, until pretty soon the whole canopy was quaking.

We spent the rest of the day moving other things with our minds: easy things like grass, sunlight, dandelion silk.

We made Mrs. Delmato blink her eyes.

We made John-John Crowley wobble on his bike.

We made Mr. Moniker's crazy old dog pee on the fire hydrant.

And then at around five o'clock, when Mr. Delmato lit the charcoal and covered his grill with hamburgers and hot dogs and Italian sausages, and called into the neighborhood that anyone who was hungry should come and get it, and the Crowleys and the Monikers and the Konings started wandering over to stand on his lawn, and Mrs. Delmato came out with ketchup bottles and plates of tomatoes and lettuce, and Heather Anne and Lucy followed behind their mother with paper plates and cups and napkins, when the charcoals got good and hot and everyone started getting excited, we made the smoke rise up into the branches so that for one single moment everything in the neighborhood was perfect.

"Ziggy!" called Nana Jean from the porch below us. "Dinnertime!"

"I've got to go," Ziggy told me. "She's really into meals. She wants to get me fat. I don't mind. Jenny wasn't all that good about remembering dinner. June Bug Jordan, this has been a truly magnificent day."

"The best day in the history of the entire earth," I said.

"Oh no," said Ziggy. "It can't be the best day in the history of the entire earth. Because tomorrow is going to be even better. Tomorrow we'll wander to the ninth dimension. Wait until I'm inside to climb down, please. That way Nana Jean won't see you."

I nodded.

"Listen to the screen door slam and then count to one hundred before you come down. Good night, June Bug Jordan."

"Good night, Ziggy Karlo," I said.

Then he climbed down with Matthew riding on his shoulder.

Ziggy crossed the lawn and stood with Nana Jean on the porch. They watched the neighbors milling around at the Delmatos' place with their paper plates full of hamburgers and potato chips. They stood around talking about neighborhood things, about teachers and taxes and lawn mowers. All the kids went out back to play on Lucy and Heather Anne's swing set.

"You want to go over there and get something to eat?" asked Nana Jean.

Buzz threw a football to John-John, who jumped and caught it.

"No way," said Ziggy.

"Good," said Nana Jean. "Because you and I have something more important to do tonight."

"What's that?" asked Ziggy.

"Well, I thought we'd give Jenny a call. See how things are going."

Ziggy's face went very still.

"I don't think so," he said.

"Don't you want to talk to your mama?"

"Oh, I *do*," said Ziggy. "I miss her so much, it's like a hole in my heart. I'm just not sure she's going to miss *me* yet. I couldn't bear it if she didn't miss me."

"Oh, Ziggy," said Nana Jean, putting her arm around him. "How did you get to be so wise?"

"Jenny says I was born that way," said Ziggy.

"I think she's right."

"Let's go in," said Ziggy.

"Okay," said Nana Jean. "In we go."

I waited for the screen door to slam just like he told me it would, and then I counted to one hundred before I climbed down.

I walked past the Delmatos' house, where all the grown-ups gathered. Lucy and Buzz and some of the other neighborhood kids were playing in the tree house, and John-John and Heather Anne were taking turns swinging on an old tire swing that hung from a tall tree. One of them would climb on so they were standing on the top of the tire, and the other one would haul them back as far as they could go and then push them hard so they swung high over the hill and then back. Heather Anne was hanging on and John-John was pushing her, and she had thrown her head back and was laughing. Her teeth were so straight and so white, and she looked so happy that something inside me broke and I started to feel mean. I started to hate Heather Anne's cute hair-sprayed feathered bangs and crimped hair and her cute Day-Glo tank top and her cute cutoff jeans and her cute straight white teeth.

I picked up a small rock from the side of the

road, and without even thinking about it, I walked across the street and hurled that rock at Heather Anne as hard as I could.

"Hey!" screamed Heather Anne, clutching her shoulder.

John-John spotted me right away and pulled a horrible face that made him look just like his brother, even though he usually was nowhere near as ugly. "June Bug Jordan threw a rock at Heather Anne!" he shouted.

All the neighborhood kids stopped playing and stared at me.

Heather Anne's face was red, and there were tears starting to stream out of her eyes. She was rubbing her shoulder.

"Why'd you do that, June Bug?" she asked.

"Hey, June Bug," said Buzz, leaping from the tree house and advancing toward me. "See what happens when you throw a rock at *me*! She won't do it. She's scared. You scared, June Bug? She won't do it. She's crazy. Everyone knows it."

"She *is* crazy," said Lucy. "But her mom's even crazier. And they all have AIDS at her house, so don't get too close or you'll get it too."

Lucy and Buzz and John-John came over to the edge of the lawn.

I picked up another rock, a bigger one this time. I gathered my magic, extended my mind, and hurled it as hard as I could at Buzz, but Buzz was so mean, the magic fizzled and the rock clattered onto the road. Buzz picked it up and ran at me, screaming, "Stay away from us, you psycho!"

I took another rock, extended my mind, and threw it as hard as I could at Buzz, who caught it this time, in one fist, and charged down the street with a rock in each hand like he was going to brain me with them.

John-John and Lucy took off behind him, screaming, "Get her! Get her!"

Heather Anne followed them.

I ran as fast as I could down Trowbridge Road, leaving Ziggy's house and the smell of the Delmatos' barbecue and all the grown-ups behind us, the sound of our feet hitting the pavement past the tall houses and all the way down to number twenty-eight, where the porch sighed, and the raspberries grew wild, and all the curtains were pulled closed so that no sunlight could come inside.

I stood in front of my house, and Buzz and John-John and Lucy and Heather Anne stood around me.

We looked at each other, not sure what to do next.

Buzz wound up like a softball pitcher.

Then, suddenly, right before he let go, there was a clattering racket coming from the top floor of the house.

We all looked up to the window and there was Mother.

She had not shown her face to anyone but me and Uncle Toby since the funeral, and now she was pushing back the curtains and glaring down at us in her white nightgown. Her tangled hair fell over her jutting shoulders. Her skeletal face stared out at us with her mouth gaping open, screaming.

"A ghost!" shrieked John-John.

"Run!" yelled Lucy. "Run as fast as you can!"

Buzz dropped his rocks.

They took off screaming back down the road toward the Delmatos' house.

They ran so hard, Buzz practically kicked himself in the butt while he ran, and John-John and Lucy were screeching about the ghost they saw at the window, and Heather Anne was crying about her shoulder, and pretty soon all four of them were surrounded by neighbors who cooed over them and made them feel like they were the ones who had been wronged.

I dodged headlong into my house, my heart still pounding in my chest, forgetting completely to slide off my sandals, forgetting completely to wipe the outdoor smells off my skin, bounding all the way up the stairs two steps a time, throwing open our bedroom door, and running in to hug my mother, who had just saved my life, but I found her wrapped in the curtains, staring at me.

Her face was white. She was not smiling at all.

Bristle Brush

"Thanks for scaring those kids away."

"You're my daughter," said Mother in a voice that sounded like broken glass.

"They thought you were a ghost. John-John Crowley was shrieking like a baby. You should have seen him."

"I saw him," said Mother.

It was the voice of a person holding her body still because she does not want to fall through ice.

"Then why are you so upset?"

Mother inhaled slowly.

"You have disgustingness all over your body. All over your body, June."

"Just on my hands," I told her. "The rest of me is okay."

"No," Mother whispered. She unwrapped herself from the curtain and edged closer, taking long shaking breaths through her nose. "It's everywhere. On your hands. In your hair. You're covered with it."

"That's an exaggeration."

"Don't talk back to me."

"I wasn't talking back."

"You were. Your mouth is dirty, and it's doing dirty things."

"I'll wash my mouth and my face. I'll brush my teeth with baking soda."

"No," said Mother. "That's not going to be enough."

"Please," I begged her, frenzy creeping its way into my voice. "I won't get dirty again. I promise. Please just let me take a nice bath. I want to take a nice bath and then get into some inside clothes. I'll smell clean. I promise I'll smell clean."

We walked to the bathroom together. Her eyes were filled with shadows.

She took a pair of surgical gloves out of the box. Then she reached under the sink and brought out a white plastic bottle of Clorox bleach and a scrub brush.

She turned on the hot water.

There was a sudden rush of current. Heat filled the tiny room with steam until my lips and my face were glazed.

She poured in three caps of the Clorox. The water began to swirl and bubble, and the scent of bleach rose into the room.

Mother sat on the edge of the tub in her night-gown.

I could see the staircase of her spine.

Silently, I put my clothes into the plastic trash bag and then tied the top so that disgustingness wouldn't seep out and reinfect me.

Mother pushed the bundle out the bathroom door with her feet. Now the bath was ready. So hot, the room swirled in steam.

I put one foot in. "It's too hot, Mother."

"I know," she said gravely. "It needs to be."

I put the other foot in.

Then I lowered myself down, grimacing as the water closed over my legs.

"Scrub it off," Mother told me. "Quick before you burn."

"It's going to hurt," I said.

"I know, sweetheart."

"I promise I won't do it again."

Mother held herself. Tears streamed down her face. "I need you to finish this. I have a clean towel waiting for you. We'll put you right in the bed. And I'll play you anything you want. Prelude. Allemande. Anything. I'll make the hurt go away."

I nodded and gritted my teeth. I scrubbed and scrubbed.

When it was over, Mother helped me stagger from the bathtub and into a clean white nightgown. She wrapped her arms around me very gently. Then she half led, half carried me to our bedroom. She laid me down on our white bed. I curled onto my side and pulled the crisp sheets to my chin, wrapping myself in the scent of clean. All at once, I was too tired to keep my eyes open. My body was raw. The sheet against my elbows and knees felt like fire. I closed my eyes and tried not to cry.

Mother took her cello out of the case, tightened the bow, pulled out the endpin, and sat on the stool by the bed. She played the Allemande with such tenderness, each note ran its fingers across my skin, each bow stroke a smooth, cool palm.

My eyes were closed in pain, so I couldn't say for certain if she was crying, but the music wept, the lines rising and falling in a whisper, and even though the key signature was G major, usually bright and optimistic, tonight it was brooding and mournful.

I would feed you if I could, said the cello in the lengthening shadows of Mother's bedroom. *I would touch you and hold you. I would open the windows and let the outside air come in. But I am made of wood. I am as trapped as you are. My foot is rooted in the ground, and I am unable to make a sound unless the woman puts her hands on me. I have no voice except for when she plays.*

It was not medicine. It was an apology.

The Allemande ended with its G major chord, two beautiful notes on the bottom and two on the top, the last one ringing into the room like sunlight.

Mother put the cello and bow back into the case and came to lie down behind me. She pulled me close, wrapped her arms around me, and breathed into my neck until she fell asleep.

I lay in front of her, curled against her grief.

My skin stung, especially in the places where I

folded, the insides of my elbows and knees, or where I touched the sheet. I lay there staring at the ceiling, using my mind to trace the crack in the plaster.

I imagined different things that could snake. A river of ink. A long, narrow scar. I lifted one hand from the blankets, closed one eye, and used my shaking finger to travel the line across the ceiling. I was an ant in a long caravan of ants, heading out of our sweltering room and into the windy distance. I was a car on the highway, inching off into nowhere.

I lifted her arm from my waist and winced as I twisted sideways, grimacing as the bedsheets glanced against my skin, squirming like a salamander from the blankets and wriggling onto the floor, hands first, then belly, then legs — so that soon I was on all fours on the floor, crouching in the dark, Mother's dream-breath hissing into the room like thread drawn through silk.

I left Mother sleeping and crawled from our room. Each heartbeat gave me more courage until it was like a drumbeat calling soldiers to war. Here she is. June Bug Jordan. Leaving the bedroom in the middle of the night to gather what she needs to break free.

Can you see her?

She is glowing there, a tiny ember, in her first moment of glory.

I crept into the hallway, where all the closed doors looked at me like sideways one-eyed faces. Daddy's study had his broken voice. My old bedroom had my little kid's voice. The yellow bedroom had the voice of my grandma, whom I only remembered in dreams, a stern woman who one time posed in a photograph inside a rose garden holding a little newborn baby that was me.

I crept to each door and whispered into the place where the door meets the threshold.

"I'll be back," I whispered into Daddy's study. I put my mouth against the keyhole and inhaled slowly, drawing his air inside my mouth, tiny particles of who he was, swirling through the keyhole and into me. It made me brave. "Hello, Daddy. I've missed you." *I've missed you too, June Bug. I've missed you too.*

And now I knew I was brave enough for the gathering. A bag filled with Necessaries, to strip myself of all future disgustingness. In the upstairs bathroom, I found most of what I needed: a box of latex gloves, a nail file, a nail clipper, a pair of scissors, a pair of tweezers, a toothbrush, some toothpaste, some mouthwash, a bar of Ivory soap, a bottle of rubbing alcohol, Q-tips, and some dental floss. These I rolled up in my white nightgown so they wouldn't fall when I padded, barefoot, down the stairs.

My empty backpack was still hanging on the hook by the pantry, a perfect home for the Necessaries. Zip. Zip. In they went.

How wonderful and how powerful I felt standing alone in my kitchen, bare feet flat and cool against the wooden floor, with my very own backpack filled with Necessaries. I searched the kitchen drawers and put in other instruments that caught my eye. A carrot scraper. A potato peeler. A cheese grater. A soup ladle. A spatula. A letter opener.

There was no disgustingness too smelly. Just a light brush of the carrot scraper would scoop germs from my skin. I could clean my fingernails with the tip of the letter opener. I could pour mouthwash over my hands, scrub it into all the cracks and crevices with the potato peeler. I could touch anyone or anything, and Mother would never know.

Oh, Backpack, you will save me.

I kissed the zipper. I kissed the strap. I kissed the

pocket in the front. Tomorrow would be the first day of my life. My new birthday.

You will wait for me, Backpack, I whispered into the pocket. *You will be here when I need you, and you will guide me all the way.*

I tiptoed to the front door and carefully opened it.

I turned the doorknob with both hands and pulled hard. I put muscle into it. And then I was standing in the dark, wet square of night with Backpack on my shoulders. I walked down the porch stairs. Cool air glazed my cheeks. I stood on the gray flagstones and raised my face, letting the outside air cover every inch of me, washing away the burn, Mother's breath, and the angry eyes of the neighborhood children.

I jumped in shadows. I twirled and laughed. I opened my mouth wide and drank in the dark, slick sidewalk, the nighttime sky, the cast-iron streetlamps, the tall, gabled houses, the maple and pine trees, and the whole ridiculous, broken world swirling inside me because it had been mine to drink all along. I closed my eyes and allowed the wind to touch my face, cool as Daddy's fingertips.

Then I tiptoed back to the front door, and carefully, carefully I opened it.

For a moment the smell of the summer night came rushing into the house along with the momentary chirping of crickets.

Not so fast.

I pushed Backpack out onto the porch. *Stay there. Don't move. I'll be back for you tomorrow.* I closed the door tight before Mother could feel the stirring of air and wake to find me gone.

I stood in the hallway a moment, my stinging body on one side of the door, and Backpack on the other. Suddenly it was as if I had an umbilical cord that linked me with the outside even when the door was closed.

There was wind blowing on the backpack. I could feel it. And even though I couldn't hear them anymore, there were cicadas singing from the trees, and Backpack was there experiencing it all, storing it up in his pockets, waiting for me to come back and drink the nighttime into my lungs.

The sky was just beginning to lighten when I finally made my way up the stairs to our bedroom, the faintest gray of morning casting a white veil across the windows. How strange to listen to Mother's snoring, knowing that my life was about to change. How strange to creep back into our four-poster bed, slide beneath the white blanket, and wrap her arms back over my belly so I could feel, once again, her mouth blowing warm, humid breath across the nape of my neck. This time, instead of lying there awake, I found myself snuggling into her, closing my eyes, and falling into a deep and dreamless sleep.

Courante

The bright sixteenth notes woke me from my sleep.

I turned my head on the pillow. Mother was playing the Courante. Her hair was undone, back-lit by the late-morning sun seeping from the cracks beneath the curtains, her white nightgown draped around the wooden chair, her bow moving across the strings. But even a piece like the Courante, a dance in the key of G that seems so hopeful when you listen to the surface of it, can hold darkness inside its mouth, tucked into the corner of its cheek like a bitter pill.

Listen to the sweetness of the notes, but don't forget that the stirring you feel, moving beneath the joy, is something more complicated. By the end of the piece, just as you are sighing at the tenderness, you realize there is also something that cannot be fixed, even after the last bright note dissolves. There is something broken in the bed, curled in the sheets, shivering despite the summer sun.

When she was finished, Mother put her cello away and helped me out of bed, carefully, gingerly, so my skin wouldn't brush against the sheets. She found me a light yellow sundress, something that could drop over my head and float around me while I moved, barely touching my burns. I winced when I lowered my arms and the dress fell into place.

"Are you going to be okay?" she asked me.

"I think so," I said.

"Your skin is going to heal. You know that, right?"

"I know," I said. "But right now, it feels like a sunburn."

She reached out to touch my cheek. "Sunburns aren't so bad, are they?"

"Just at first," I told her. "Just at the creases where your skin folds."

"I never wanted to hurt you," Mother said. "I only wanted to protect you."

"I know," I said. "I know, Mommy."

"Are you hungry for breakfast?"

"I'm always hungry."

She kissed the top of my head with dry lips.

"Let's go," she told me. "I want to see you eat."

Mother took my wrist and led me down to the kitchen, from the sink to the pantry to the refrigerator to the stove, moving my fingers to crack the eggs and stir, to chop the onions and peppers. She even sat at the table with me and ate a few small bites herself, chewing slowly, watching me, trying to smile. I could feel the chair on the backs of my legs. Outside the window, Mr. Moniker's old hound dog was barking at the wind. I could hear the voices of the neighborhood kids playing on the street in front of our house.

"Mother," I said. "There is something important I have to tell you."

"Yes, my sweet girl."

"I'm sorry for coming home with so much disgustingness on me last night. I know it hurts you when I get dirty. I have decided that I'm never going to get dirty again. I want you to be happy, Mommy.

Please forgive me." I reached for her across the table.

"Oh, honey." Mother clasped my hands. "Do you know how much I love you?"

"Yes."

She kissed my fingers. "Do you *really* know? Or are you just saying it? Oh, June, I hope you really *do* know it. Deep inside where it counts."

"I know it deep down inside. I'm not just saying that. I really do."

"Daddy would be so proud of you."

"Do you think so?" I asked.

"Oh yes, June," Mother said. She looked me full in my face. "Oh my goodness, yes." She reached onto the windowsill with one hand and pulled down the last photograph anyone ever took of our family while it was still whole.

I came to her side and we leaned in together.

Here was Mother, smiling with teeth so white, she almost seemed a child herself, her hair long and flowing, her face unlined. It was the night of her Carnegie Hall concert. She was wearing a gown that fell gently around her body, and she had curves, which meant there was flesh under the clothing. I was standing next to her, my hair in braids. And here was Daddy standing behind us with his beautiful face and his long eyelashes and his tall, healthy body. He was wearing his patchwork coat. His graceful hands were resting on our shoulders. He was not smiling. He was biting his lips to keep all the secrets from coming out.

"You look a lot like him, you know," Mother said.

I nodded, biting my lips. I had secrets too.

Now Mother rubbed her cheek against the top of my head. She smelled my scalp. I could feel her breath on my head.

"Mother," I said in a small voice.

She kept on breathing through her nose. I could hear air whistling through her sinuses.

"Mother," I said again, this time louder.

Then I pulled away.

We looked at each other. Her eyes were wide.

"I am going out to play now," I told her. "I promise not to get any disgustingness on me. Everything is going to be okay. I promise. I love you so much, Mommy."

"I love you too," she said.

I left her in the kitchen with the picture of our unbroken family in her hands.

What did she see when I walked away from her?

The back of my head, moving into the distance? How did she breathe when I opened the front door and let myself out?

Backpack was waiting for me, just where I left him the night before. The Necessaries were huddled inside, waiting.

They jangled when I swung Backpack onto my shoulder, and I winced as he brushed against my skin, but it was okay because instead of being the pain of a captive, it was the pain of a soldier.

I was a soldier in the jungle with a pack of ammunition. Guns and knives and bombs that looked like little pineapples. Backpack clanged against my body while I marched down Trowbridge Road. Past Lucy and Heather Anne sitting on their front steps with their boom box tuned to the summer hits. Past John-John and Buzz throwing acorns at cars as they drove by. I marched with my tweezers and nail file and carrot scraper. Metallic and musical as a hurdy-gurdy. My bag full of Necessaries. A good kind of pain.

Ziggy was waiting in the copper beech tree, leaning against the trunk, his long red hair pulled into a braid. Matthew the ferret was perched on the top of his head. I unshouldered Backpack at the base of the tree and scrambled up the way I always did, wincing when I bent my arms and knees, but feeling strong as I stepped with purpose onto the first burl, pulling onto the first branch, swinging my leg over, and scrambling up.

"June Bug Jordan," said Ziggy, smiling, "I am really glad you came back."

Matthew uncurled from Ziggy's head and scratch-scrambled down his braid, across his legs, and over to me, chattering excitedly, his white tail all puffed up. I reached out and brought the ferret to my nose. He smelled musky and wild. I kissed him on the top of the head.

"I wasn't sure you would want to see me again today," said Ziggy.

"Why wouldn't I want to see you?"

"I don't know," said Ziggy. "Most people have had enough after one time, and you have already had two, so I figured maybe that was it."

"Well, that's just silly," I said. "We're friends now, aren't we?"

"We are," said Ziggy. "And friends always come back."

"Friends always come back," I agreed. "Especially magic best friends like us."

Ziggy smiled. "Magic best friends," he said. "I

like the sound of that." But then his eyes looked worried. "Hey," he said, suddenly, leaning closer. "What happened?"

"What do you mean?"

"Your face. Your skin. You're all red."

"I spent too much time in the sun," I told him.

Ziggy glared at me accusingly. "Yesterday you were with me. We were in the shade."

"It was from last week. My uncle Toby took me to Cape Cod. I forgot to bring suntan lotion."

"You are lying to me," said Ziggy. "Sunburns don't last a week."

"Mine do," I said.

Ziggy was silent.

"Maybe it's the dress," he offered finally.

"The dress?"

"Yes," said Ziggy. "I never saw you in a dress before. Maybe the yellow makes your skin look pinker. Like when you hold a buttercup under your chin."

"That's probably it," I said, relieved. "This is my dress for my first time traveling in the ninth dimension. I'm glowing because I'm ready. Can you see? The magical beasts in the ninth dimension have been waiting for me to appear with my skin glowing beneath this yellow dress made of honey and sunlight."

"*You* are made of honey and sunlight," said Ziggy, looking sideways at me.

"And *you* are made of lemons."

"And mint," said Ziggy. "And also dandelion silk, ferret musk, and milkweed. Huzzah!"

"Are you ready to wander between the shadows?" I asked him.

"June Bug Jordan," he said, "I have never been more ready for anything in my life."

Majestica

I climbed down first, and Ziggy followed close behind me. We went burl by burl, hand over hand, until our feet reached the ground and we could sneak past the porch, where Nana Jean sat in the chair with her macramé owl and pretended not to notice as I pulled Ziggy behind the house into her garden.

Vegetables were sprouting everywhere. There were rows of snap peas stretching their necks, and the leafy green vines of cherry tomatoes. There were the low, lobed leaves of cucumber plants spilling over the edges of the garden. Down the hill was the orchard, where there were too many yellow peaches, hard and proud and covered in fuzz. There were a hundred promises of apples so heavy already that the trees bent and sighed.

We ducked past the boxwood on the edge of Nana Jean's property, and that is when we first caught a glimpse of the ninth dimension. Below us, we could see the grassy basin that everyone said used to be a farm a long time ago, but now was just a weird, empty hollow with crumbled bricks and a stone foundation rising from the ground, and tall grass no one ever mowed growing wild everywhere over mounds of half-buried treasure—the yawning mouth of a blue milk bottle, a bicycle tire, the handle of a cracked water jug.

"Can you see it?" said Ziggy, and he gestured with his long arm at what belonged to me. "All of this has been waiting for you since the day you were born."

Here was an old hollow log that was absolutely covered with shelf mushrooms. Here was a mound of dandelions, and over there was a cellar hole filled with pine needles and brown leaves that smelled like cinnamon.

"It belongs to us," said Ziggy. "This place. The ninth dimension. No one can hurt us here."

We ran together toward the place that looked the most magical: the cellar hole. There were four crumbled walls of gray fieldstones and, down below, the wet smell of summer leaves. "This is going to be our sanctuary," I told him.

"I love it," said Ziggy.

"Let's find sticks to make a canopy so that if it rains, we can be safe."

"Okay," said Ziggy. "Good idea."

We scouted for fallen branches. Some were still new and covered with green leaves, and some had been on the ground for so long that the bark had fallen away and the branches were more like wizard staves, white and smooth as bone. These were my favorites because they felt good to touch, and if I scratched one fingernail into the flesh of the wood, I could carve magical runes that shone from deep inside.

Soon we had covered most of the cellar hole with branches, but we left an opening in one corner wide enough for us to lower ourselves down feetfirst. I led and Ziggy followed with Matthew on his shoulder, chattering and bristling as we descended into the brand-new not-quite darkness. I pulled him into the far corner, and we huddled together in the shadows, breathing in the scent of wet leaves and pine needles. There was filtered light shining through the cracks between the branches, and through the open corner where we entered there was a single shaft of golden light casting patterns on the leafy ground. Matthew leapt from Ziggy's shoulder and started dancing on tiptoes between the shadows. He whirled in circles and zoomed back and forth from one end of the sanctuary to the other.

"This sanctuary needs a name," said Ziggy.

"It has a name," I told him. "It's called Majestica."

Ziggy rose to his feet and spread his arms. He had to duck his head so he wouldn't hit it against the branches, but when he spoke, his voice was proud and deep. "By the power of the ninth dimension and Majestica, I ask you now, wandering nomad, are you ready to claim your powers?"

"Yes," I said.

Matthew bounced and bristled in joyous agreement.

I took handfuls of wet leaves from the ground

and rubbed them all over my face, across my forehead, and down each of my cheeks. I wove them into my hair. I chose one wet leaf and put it in my mouth. It tasted like rain and earth.

Then I rose. I fit perfectly inside Majestica. I didn't even have to duck my head.

Light streamed in from between the branches.

"Come on," I said. "It's time for the ceremony."

Ziggy stepped aside so I could go first. We crept to the empty corner, climbing up the stones and hoisting ourselves back outside into the ninth dimension, where everything looked different, somehow, now that it really belonged to me. Here were the remains of an old shoe, and here was the crumbling foundation of the barn, and here was the hollow log, and the bicycle tire, and the handle of a broken water jug, and the same tall grass growing wild, but somehow it was shimmering now and all the details were filtered in a golden light.

"It's beautiful," I whispered.

"That's because you're seeing the magic," said Ziggy. "Mortals only see a hundredth of what's real. We are better than them."

Something crackled and thrummed behind us.

We turned and looked. There was a golden glow emanating from deep inside Majestica. We could see it shining up through the branches, a strange pulsing light.

"It's Matthew," said Ziggy. "We left him down there."

Something rumbled and roared.

"That doesn't sound like Matthew," I said.

"That's because we're in the ninth dimension. Any nomad who wants to transform can do it. Matthew loves changing. Look what happens next. Matthew won't be Matthew anymore."

Soon I discovered that this was both true and not true, because when Matthew rose from the empty corner of Majestica and into the air before us, we could see that his body was still long and lean and ferret-like, but now, instead of being covered in fine white fur, he was covered in iridescent scales, and he had a bristling white tail, and wings that were made of white fire, and he crackled into the air like a firework, twirling and spluttering somersaults. Then he hissed at us with his mouth wide open and disappeared into the vast blue sky.

"I want to do that," I told Ziggy.

"Go ahead," Ziggy told me. "All you have to do is wish and it will become true."

Ziggy put his arms out to demonstrate.

I put my arms out too.

Suddenly, we catapulted into the clouds, our fire-breath flaring red and orange. We opened our mouths so that heaven could stream down our throats. There were clouds all around us, billowing, filled with shimmering feathers.

"See that ocean of clouds over there?" I asked Ziggy, pointing to a place in the sky where they rippled like waves.

"I see it," said Ziggy.

"I can make that whole ocean disappear if I want to," I told him. "All I have to do is shriek the highest note I can and it will explode."

"Shriek away," said Ziggy.

I rose to the top of the cumulus cloud.

Below me was the ninth dimension.

I could see it so far away that it hardly seemed real. I took a very deep breath. Then I closed my eyes, opened my mouth, and shrieked with all my might. The highest note my voice could make exploded from my lungs and shook the sky. I shrieked and shrieked. I closed my eyes and let it come all the way up from my toes.

Then the sound changed and things started coming out of the shriek that I didn't expect: Daddy biting his lips. Mother's tears. All the locked doors.

My tummy, hungry and empty, drinking its own emptiness.

The loneliness of Mother's bedroom.

The sound of her cello.

I shrieked and shrieked, and tears rolled down my face.

It was too much. The tears were too heavy, and I couldn't stay in the air with all this sadness filling my lungs. I sank below the clouds, through the air, and back down to earth, where I dropped to my knees and wept. Ziggy and Matthew sank with me. Ziggy stayed by my side the entire time. He didn't try to wipe away my tears or to hush me or tell me it was okay. He just sat next to me and let my sadness take the time it needed.

"June Bug," he whispered finally, when my crying turned into shuddering gasps and then, finally, just silent tears. "June Bug. Look up at the sky. Look at what your shrieking did."

I tilted my head back and opened my eyes.

It looked like someone had punched a hole through the clouds.

There was a startling burst of blue sky coming through, the edges dissolving into thin white wisps.

"Huzzah," said Ziggy. "June Bug Jordan did that."

I rubbed my eyes. My face felt red and hot. My head ached from all the shrieking.

I put my head into my hands.

I felt like I might break.

Ziggy patted my back to comfort me. It burned. I winced and pulled away.

"That hurts?" asked Ziggy.

I nodded.

"It's not really a sunburn, is it?" said Ziggy.

I shook my head.

"Someone did this to you?"

"No," I said quietly. "I did it to myself."

"Why would you do something like this to yourself?"

"I can't tell you," I said. "It's not something I talk about."

I looked at him, my eyes so filled with secrets that they burned.

"I understand," said Ziggy. "I have things I don't talk about, either."

"I think I'm ready to go back," I told him.

Ziggy helped me up, and I leaned against him as we walked slowly, slowly, out of the ninth dimension, leaving the stone foundations and the cellar hole and grassy hollow behind us.

We headed back up the hill and past the boxwoods, through the orchard, and into Nana Jean's early summer garden, where the vegetables were still filled with all their first green juice.

Nana Jean did not say a word as we stole past the porch and back to the copper beech tree, where Backpack was waiting for me, filled with Necessaries that clinked and clanged when Ziggy lifted him and helped me swing him up to my shoulder again. I winced as the weight of the backpack pulled against my skin.

"You sure you're okay?" Ziggy asked.

I nodded. "I'm better than I was before," I said.

"Meet me here tomorrow," said Ziggy. "And we can go back to Majestica. If you want to shriek again, you can shriek. And if you want to fly some more, we can fly. Anything you want. We'll do it."

"Why are you so nice to me?" I asked him.

"I don't know," said Ziggy. "Maybe because you remind me of me."

Ziggy put the ferret back on his head and walked off toward the porch, where Nana Jean was waiting for him.

I watched him go.

I knelt on the ground and unzipped Backpack's mouth.

I pulled the carrot scraper from the bottom of his mouth. It was silver and shiny.

I feather-dusted the carrot scraper across my palms, stripping away the thinnest, thinnest particles of skin so she would never know I had been so close to another person.

That's better. Nice clean skin.

Then I took out the rubbing alcohol.

I wet three fingers and rubbed it across my lips.

My lips tingled, but that was okay.

Then I took out the toothpaste and mouthwash.

I mixed the toothpaste and mouthwash into the cap and stirred it with a stick.

Then I poured the minty mixture into my mouth and gargled with it.

I spit.

Fresh.

Burning fresh.

I untangled the leaves from my hair; I brushed the dirt off my face; I flossed my fingernails and put Q-tips up my nose to swab out the tree bark.

Now it was time for my legs and arms and face.

What should I use? Scissors? Too snippy.

Ivory soap? Too pure.

I took out Letter Opener and opened his blade. He was silver and shining faintly in the sunlight.

Look at that. I am a pretty girl. Look at my big blue eyes.

Letter Opener winked at me and gleamed mischievously. He wanted a turn.

I dropped him into Backpack. Some guys can be so bossy.

Rubbing alcohol. That is the best thing.

I splashed a cupful over my hands and smoothed it over my bare arms and legs and face, rubbing it because why else would it be called rubbing alcohol, dummy.

It tingled. Nice and cool.

Now I could smell my new self. I did not smell like Ziggy. I did not smell like a ferret or like leaves or earth. I smelled like a hospital room. Perfect for Mother.

I put the Necessaries into Backpack's mouth and zipped them all the way up.

I trudged home with Backpack clattering behind me, filled with everything I needed to be free. When I got home, I kicked off my sandals, leaned Backpack against the wall of the porch, and let myself in. Then I closed the door behind me fast, so that none of the glorious, dirty, wonderfully infected outside air could make its way inside. It was my very own secret. Gleaming somewhere just out of reach.

Swallow the Moon

It was scratched and scuffed and chipped along the edges, and its steel strings jutted out from the tuning pegs like gray whiskers on a lonesome alley cat. Uncle Toby played the blues with his eyes closed tight, his long, dark lashes resting like crow's feathers on his cheeks.

It was hot and muggy inside, the way it sometimes can be in the middle of July when the sun is fierce and nothing seems to be moving except the mosquitoes. But the sun was going down, and there was a breeze now. The sky was dark with storm clouds coming. We sat back-to-back on the front porch so I could feel his voice vibrating against my shoulder blades, Uncle Toby with his scratched-up guitar and me savoring my sandwich, his gentle notes soothing all the places that hurt. I ate the sandwich and listened to the voice that was so similar to my daddy's voice, I could almost close my eyes and forget which man was sitting behind me. They had the same soft-slippered consonants, as though their tongues were tiptoeing while they sang, dancing across velvet.

"Did you and my daddy ever play music together?" I asked him while he strummed and fingerpicked up and down the fingerboard. "I bet it would've sounded pretty."

"Nah," said Uncle Toby. "I don't think your dad ever even knew I played guitar."

"How could he not have known?"

"I was five years younger," said Uncle Toby. "By the time I was a teenager, your daddy was already in college. He barely knew I existed."

"I bet that wasn't true," I said. "I bet he would have loved playing with you if you had asked him."

"He was so serious, he never would have wanted to mess around with someone like me. He had real talent. I just kind of noodle around by ear, you know? I'm nothing compared to what he was."

Uncle Toby kept on playing, fingerpicking up and down the fingerboard. Then he started to sing:

Sittin' on the porch with the sun in my eyes
Sittin' on the porch with no clouds in the skies
Sittin' with my June Bug, singing a tune
Singin' to the stars and the silvery moon

"You could have been a musician too," I told him.

"Maybe," said Uncle Toby, laughing. "But I never really put my mind to it. Your daddy was the one who always cared about doing things right. I never knew what I wanted to do with my life. Never wanted to go to college. Never wanted to settle down. Guess the lumberyard's good enough for someone like me. Flexible hours. Time outdoors. The smell of wood on my hands. Not bad, all things considered."

Uncle Toby pushed me a little with his elbow and then started playing again.

Sittin' on the front porch, sun in my face
Sweet sun shinin' all over the place

Hungry little June Bug, singin' a tune
Hungry little June Bug, swallow the moon

He put the guitar down, and we turned so we were sitting side by side instead of back-to-back. I pushed his knee with my knee, and he pushed my knee with his.

"No one's ever made up a song about me," I said. "Not even my daddy."

"Honey," said Toby, smiling, "you *were* his song. You were what he loved and what he was most proud of in the whole entire world."

"What about my mom?" I asked.

"What about her?"

"Didn't he love her?"

"Didn't he what?"

"Didn't he *love* her? Didn't he love my mom?"

Sometimes I was surprised at the force of my own voice. This was one of those times—my words were so sharp and straight, they were almost like arrows.

"Well, of course he loved your mom," said Uncle Toby. "They played duets together. Him on the piano and her on the cello. And they had these long talks. I think your mom was the first person in this world your dad could really talk to. He loved that about her. I'll never forget when he brought her home for Christmas that first year. We all took one look at them and we just knew."

"What did you just know?"

"Well, we knew things were going to change, I guess. He had found himself a girl. Your grandma couldn't have been happier. We knew your daddy was probably going to ask your mom to marry him, and we knew she was going to say yes."

"Because they loved each other?"

"Because they loved each other," said Uncle Toby, looking me straight in the eye. "And then they graduated from the conservatory and you came on the scene, and they moved into this house to take care of you and to help out your grandma. And this was a house so full of love again, it just made everyone feel warm and welcome, so I came over for dinner a lot more, and it was a good time for us. Do you still remember your grandma?"

I nodded, even though my memories were hazy, and I was never sure if they were real or imaginary. They came from photographs. A silver cross. A rose garden. A hard face. Warm arms. Laughter. A pretty singing voice like both her boys. Not much more than that. But what more do you need?

"She loved having you in this house," Uncle Toby said. "She loved all the baby noises you made. All the coos and gurgles. She loved seeing your daddy holding you. And then she passed away, and you grew up into this beautiful girl, and as long as you're here in this house, all that love just lasts and lasts." He leaned over and kissed me on the head.

"How come you never came back to live with Grandma?"

Uncle Toby sighed. Sometimes telling the truth makes you weary.

"I liked being on my own, I guess," he said. "That's how it's been since I was old enough to take care of myself. Besides, your grandma and me, we never really saw eye to eye about things."

"What kind of things?"

"Well," said Uncle Toby, "I guess about religion and politics mostly. Your grandma was very old-fashioned and set in her ways. She had strong ideas about how a person should and shouldn't live their life."

"Did my daddy see eye to eye with her?"

Uncle Toby smiled at me. "Well," he said. "No. He didn't. Not at all. But your daddy would never have done anything to hurt your grandma. He loved her too much. And he was always her angel. But me, I guess I've always been a little rebellious."

"I'm like you," I said.

Uncle Toby tousled my hair. "That's one of the things I like about you," he said. "We can be rebels together."

I ate the final bite of my sandwich and wiped my hands on my legs. There was a question scratching at the back of my head, and I wasn't sure it was polite to ask, but if I didn't I would be itchy the rest of my life, so I took a breath and asked it.

"Now that Grandma's gone, does it ever make you feel bad that we live in your old house and you live in an apartment far away?"

Uncle Toby looked me right in the face. "June Bug," he said. "As long as you're here in this house, it's all worth it. As long as you are growing up healthy and safe and sound, I don't feel bad one bit."

I wasn't quite sure if I truly believed his words, but they were nice to hear anyway, and for now my tummy and my heart were full, even if I hadn't swallowed any moons today.

"You know what I've been thinking about lately?" Uncle Toby asked me, sort of smiling.

"What?"

"I've been thinking about how nice it would be if I lived nearer to you. I was thinking of how long it takes for me to drive to Newton all the way from Somerville, especially when there's traffic, and how nice it would be for both of us if I lived closer."

"That *would* be nice," I said, leaning my head against his shoulder.

"I can't afford to buy a house in Newton, but I've been looking for apartments," said Uncle Toby. "I wanted to tell you that. I've been looking to see if there's something I could rent near you. That way I could come more often. I could bring you more food."

"You could play me more songs," I said.

"Right," said Uncle Toby. Then he looked behind him at the house. "I'm not sure how happy your mom would be about that. I think she's a little like your grandma was. She prefers me farther away."

"She prefers everyone farther away," I said.

Uncle Toby reached over and tousled my hair. But then his face was really serious. "Can I ask you something?"

"Sure."

"Does your mom eat anything these days?"

"Not really."

"Next time I come over, we'll get her eating."

"Okay," I whispered. "That would be good."

"I have a big shipment of lumber I need to drive out to New Jersey, so I'll be gone a couple of days. But when I come back, we'll give it a try. Things are going to get better, June Bug."

I didn't know what to say so I just sighed. Sometimes telling the truth makes you weary.

We went back-to-back again. I could feel his strong shoulders behind me, holding me up. He smelled like leather and wood chips and peppermint. I leaned my head back against him and closed my eyes.

Uncle Toby picked up the guitar and sang one more verse. I could feel his song warm on my back, humming like a heartbeat.

Swallow the moon, swallow the moon
Hungry little mongoose, swallow the moon.

Mother and Child

Ziggy and I met at the copper beech tree every day. Every single day, he was there waiting for me. I climbed up the trunk to him burl by burl. We performed the inspiration spell. And then we traveled to the ninth dimension together, where we shape-shifted and became vast, flinging our powers and our voices into the universe. But then one overcast Thursday, Ziggy wasn't there. Jenny's old car was parked in front of Nana Jean's house. The windows were rolled down, and the car seemed to yawn in the fading sun. It smelled like old cigarettes and trouble.

I climbed the copper beech tree by myself and waited for something to happen. I could hear voices inside Nana Jean's house, high and tight and filled with hurt. I could hear the sound of hurried footsteps. Then the screen door slammed, and Jenny stormed onto the porch with a laundry basket filled with her clothes. Ziggy trailed behind her with the albino ferret quivering on his shoulder and tears streaming down his face.

I held on to the branch and watched, silently.

Ziggy tried to pull Jenny back into the house and she tripped. Laundry toppled all over the porch. Jenny swore and dropped to her knees, feeling around her like a blind woman for her clothes. Ziggy crouched beside her. They picked up the laundry together. Jenny rolled each piece in a ball and shoved it back into the basket. Ziggy picked up a pair of her jeans and handed them to her. Jenny sighed and took them. Ziggy picked up one of her tie-dyed T-shirts, leaned his face into it, closed his eyes, and breathed in. Jenny took the shirt from him, rolled it into a ball, and shoved it back in the basket.

"Why can't I come home with you?" asked Ziggy so softly, I almost couldn't hear.

"You can't. It's too much right now."

"Not to stay overnight or anything. Not for dinner. Just for an hour or two. To help put the laundry away. Just a quick visit. You never said I wasn't allowed to visit."

"I keep telling you," said Jenny. "I'm not ready. Me and Donny, we have things we need to work out. Everything's still a mess."

They both rose to their feet.

"I like mess," said Ziggy. "I've lived with mess my entire life."

"That's the point," said Jenny. "You shouldn't have to. Nana's right. You need Trowbridge Road. After that horrible year we had. Those boys at school. All the trouble between me and Donny. Ziggy, honey, you don't need *me* right now. You need *this*."

"Why do you think that *you* know what I need and I *don't*?" Ziggy stomped his foot.

"Because I'm your mother," said Jenny.

"Then act like it," shouted Ziggy, right in her face. "Act like a mother and take me home."

I hugged the trunk of the copper beech tree.

Jenny took a cigarette from her pocket and lit it with shaking hands. She took a long, trembling drag.

"*Please,*" said Ziggy. "For just a few hours. I want to see my room. I want to see my books. I miss my books."

"Nana Jean has money," said Jenny. "She can buy you *new* books."

"It's not the same!" screamed Ziggy. "Don't you know it's not the *same*?!"

Across the street, Mrs. Delmato closed her kitchen windows.

There was the sound of a dog barking.

"It's not supposed to be the same, Ziggy. Everyone decided you needed a change. Your teachers, your principal, Nana Jean. And I agree with them. I know it's hard, but for once I'm doing what's right for you. This is what you need."

"But no one asked *me* what *I* wanted. How can you know what I need if you never asked me what I wanted?"

There was a crash of dishes inside the house and a low voice muttering.

Jenny turned behind her and yelled into the open window. "Mama?" she called. "Mama, I know you're listening to all this. You want to come out here and put in your two cents? You have something you want to say?"

Nana Jean came out on the porch. "You want my two cents?" she asked, wiping her hands on her apron. "You want my two cents all of a sudden?"

"Yes," said Jenny. "I want you to tell Ziggy that this change is for his own good. That he needs to stay here with you. That we discussed it all civil and quiet, and we agreed that this is what's best for him."

"You sure you want my two cents?"

"Didn't I just say I did?"

Nana Jean took a deep breath and put her hands on her hips. "Okay. Well, my two cents are that you deciding to come over here to do your laundry like a teenager and then just leaving after an hour when this boy hasn't seen you for weeks is cruel. It's just plain cruel, Jenny."

"My washing machine is broken," said Jenny. "I don't have money for the Laundromat."

Ziggy dropped onto the wicker chair. He put his head in his hands.

Nana Jean pushed Jenny closer to her son.

Jenny stumbled toward him. "Also, I wanted to see you, Ziggy. Okay? I missed you bad. And I have something for you. A present. Something I didn't get the chance to give you yet. How can I give you a present when you're yelling at me and carrying on like this? There isn't enough time. There just isn't enough time."

"Then stay for dinner, like I said when you called," Nana Jean told her. "Stay for dinner and visit with us for a while so Ziggy can spend some time with you. This here is no good. This way is just a tease for him."

"I told you, I can't stay for dinner," said Jenny, taking another drag on her cigarette.

"Why not?"

"Because," said Jenny. "Because I can't. I can't. That's all."

"You need to eat, don't you?"

"Not your cooking," said Jenny.

Nana Jean gasped like she had been slapped.

Ziggy hugged his knees and tried to make himself even smaller.

Jenny knelt down in front of the rocking chair.

"Hey, Ziggy. You want to see what I brought you? Want to see your present? I brought you a present because I love you, Goo Goo Boy, and I miss you so bad. Isn't that nice? Didn't I do a good thing?"

"You've got to stop teasing this boy," said Nana Jean. "You've got to stop ripping his heart open."

"He's my kid," said Jenny. "No one said I couldn't see him."

"You can't come and go like it's nothing," said Nana Jean. "You gotta think about *him*."

"You think it's nothing to me? It's not nothing. It's everything. Ziggy's still my Goo Goo Boy. Aren't you, Ziggy? Aren't you the Walrus? Where's my high slide? Don't you have a high slide for your Jenny anymore?"

Ziggy held himself.

Jenny reached beneath her hair and unclasped her necklace. It was made of glass beads of every color and size and shape. "I wanted you to have this," said Jenny. "I thought it would look good on you. All your red hair. Just like mine. If you lift your head from your knees a second, I can put it on you. Lift your head just a little, would you, Ziggy?"

He didn't lift his head, but he did put his hand out.

Jenny dropped the necklace into his open hand. She curled his fingers closed with her own hand. Then she kissed his fist.

"Okay," said Jenny. "I better go."

Ziggy started shaking.

Nana Jean came behind the boy and put her hands on his shoulders.

Jenny stood up.

"Goodbye, Mama," she said.

Nana Jean didn't say anything. She just hugged Ziggy tight.

"I said, goodbye."

"Goodbye, Jenny," said Nana Jean, not even looking up.

"Okay," said Jenny. "Okay, I'm going."

Jenny hoisted the laundry basket onto her hip.

Then she made her way down the stairs and into the car.

Jenny put the laundry basket into the passenger seat and walked around to the driver's side. She got in, started the engine, and turned on the radio. She sat there in the car for a second or two, just smoking her cigarette and looking out into the neighborhood. Then she sighed, stubbed the cigarette against the side of the door, and threw the wasted butt into the grass. She stepped on the gas and made her way down Trowbridge Road and on through town, the sky getting darker and the radio growing softer as she drove away.

"Why don't you come in with me?" Nana Jean said, still resting her cheek on the boy's hair. "I can make us some lunch and we can turn on the television and try to get our minds off all this. How about it? Watch a little bit of *The Price Is Right*. We can start this day over again."

"No thank you," said Ziggy into his knees. "I think I'll stay out here awhile."

Nana Jean looked into the sky.

"It's going to rain."

"Please," said Ziggy. "I just need to be alone."

"Okay," said Nana Jean. "Okay, my sweet boy." She kissed him on the top of his head. Then she wiped her face, rubbed her hands on her apron, and walked with heavy steps back into the house.

Ziggy held himself for a long time in the wicker rocking chair. When he finally uncurled, his face was red and his eyes were swollen. He opened his fist. Jenny's glass beads lay in his hand like a colorful snake. He touched them. All the colors and shapes. He rubbed the necklace against his cheek. Then he sighed, unclasped it, and put it on. Matthew muttered faintly, moving aside as Ziggy lifted his hair.

Ziggy walked down the porch steps and across the lawn to the copper beech tree.

He looked up into the branches and found me waiting for him.

I raised one hand to greet him, sadly.

There was no need for words.

He knew I had been there. He knew I had seen the whole thing.

He nodded gravely to me, and then I watched him place Matthew on his head and climb up our tree—one hand, one foot, another hand, another foot—until he could pull himself onto the branch and sit beside me in silence. He leaned against me, his face against my shoulder, while the clouds gathered. High up in the tree, where the branches crisscrossed above us, the leaves flickered copper and silver as wind blew its warm and heavy breath across their palms.

Summer Storm

I'm not sure how long we stayed that way, just sitting side by side, trying to let all that hurt lift from our skin. Ziggy's tears came easy like memories often do, just passing through like storm clouds in a summer sky, but mostly he stayed still and breathed, leaning against my shoulder, letting the sad take as long as it needed. When he had finally cried everything that needed to come out, Ziggy wiped his eyes with his sleeve and raised his head toward the darkening sky. I could see Jenny's beads around his neck, green and purple and red like strange mismatched gems.

"I like what she gave you," I said softly.

"Me too," said Ziggy. "But she was lying when she said she was planning on giving it to me all along. Jenny never plans anything. She just made that up on the spot so I would feel like she loves me. Sometimes they love you, but they don't know how to make it stick. Nana Jean told me that."

"Nana Jean knows what she's talking about," I said, trying to sound sure even though my own thoughts were swirling. "She's had lots of practice with kids and grandkids and neighbors and things."

"You're right," Ziggy said. "I just wish Jenny would figure it out for herself one of these days. You'd think with Nana Jean as her mama, she would have figured out the right way to love."

"I guess some people just take a while to learn things," I said.

"I guess so," said Ziggy.

We were both quiet for a bit, just thinking our own thoughts.

"Does your mother miss you when you're gone?" Ziggy asked me finally.

"Oh yes," I said.

"How do you know?"

"She tells me. She says I'm the best part of her day."

"Jenny never says anything like that to me," said Ziggy. "She's always got things on her mind. When I call, she says she can't talk long because Donny's there. Donny doesn't like it when she pays too much attention to me."

"Who is Donny?" I asked.

"Her boyfriend. He's been in and out my whole life. When he's around, things get very bad."

"I'm sorry," I said.

"Me too," said Ziggy.

The air was heavy. The wind blew the leaves of the copper beech tree. The sky was dark with storm clouds. Ziggy made his cloud the color of ships lost at sea. I made mine the color of fury and clapped my hands. Suddenly, there was a deep crescendo. A drum roll of thunder that swelled through the neighborhood.

Ziggy raised his arms like a conductor. The wind swelled.

Ziggy looked at me and gave me a sudden lopsided smile.

He clenched his fists to the sky and summoned another kettledrum of thunder, echoing deep in our bellies. When he waved his fist, there was a flash of lightning. And then the rain came down, barely a mist at first, then transforming into finger snaps, clipping and clattering, flicking across our faces, and soon the whole neighborhood was filled with booming, resonant applause.

I raised my arms and wiggled my fingers into the clouds.

"Come, lightning! Come, lightning, you beautiful beast!"

There was a second shattering, closer this time. The sky blanched.

And then another report of thunder.

"Let's go to the ninth dimension and conduct the storm from there," I said.

"Okay," said Ziggy.

We scurried down the wet trunk, our feet and hands slipping from the familiar handholds, slick and treacherous from rain.

Just before I found the safety of the ground, my foot slipped and I fell to my knees.

I held my knee up and let the rain pour down on it.

The blood washed away.

Soon my whole body was rain-soaked.

I swung Backpack up on my shoulders. We ran through the rain together, the Necessaries clattering on my back. I pulled Ziggy behind the house to the garden. Rain made the garden smell delicious, the scent of summer earth rising from the tomato beds. Matthew stood on Ziggy's shoulder and snuffled at the sky, shaking rain from his head. We charged past the orchard, where the apple and peach trees bowed their heads. We dodged past the boundary of the boxwoods and down the hill to the ninth dimension, where we stood on top of a pile of stones.

Ziggy raised his red face to the sky and let the rain pour down on it.

"Oh, summer storm. It is your son, Sigmund Karlo."

Ziggy screamed his words into the sky.

"Come sing your storm song for us. I command thee."

There was a flash of lightning.

The rain came harder.

Ziggy stomped his feet on the ground.

There was another clap of thunder.

I raised my arms like a conductor in front of an

orchestra. When I gave the signal, the winds blew harder. Then I stabbed the sky with my finger.

We shook our fists, and the storm clattered back. Raindrops slapped our cheeks.

There was another clap of thunder, closer now, and the rain came harder.

Matthew squealed and leapt from Ziggy's shoulder, scurrying headlong into Majestica, where he dove into the opening and disappeared.

We jumped from the pile of stones and followed Matthew into the opening, then we lowered ourselves into the darkness. It was perfectly dry on the far side of the hole. We could see the rain coming down, splashing across the stones. We leaned our backs against the far wall and caught our breath. I unshouldered Backpack and squeezed out the rain. Matthew peeked up from a pile of leaves. Then he twirled in circles and dove back underneath.

"This is a good shelter," said Ziggy.

I nodded.

The storm raged above us. The world smelled like leaves and dirt.

"I could live here," I said.

"You do live here," said Ziggy. "This is your home."

"No," I said, burying my hands in the leaves. "I mean for real."

"You would need some furniture," said Ziggy.

"Maybe just a blanket," I said. "And a pillow. I could sleep here if I ever needed a place to hide."

"Why would you need a place to hide?" asked Ziggy.

"I don't know," I said. "Nomads need to hide sometimes, don't they?"

I lay back in the leaves. I could hear the storm all around us, but inside Majestica we were safe and dry. There was enough room to stretch out my arms and legs, but it felt better to curl into a ball. I was like a coin in a warm pocket.

That's when we heard Nana Jean's voice calling.

"Ziggy!"

She must have been standing on the edge of the boxwoods.

"Ziggy? Are you okay? Ziggy, where are you? Come on inside now!"

"You better go," I said. "Nana Jean's going to worry."

"Ziggy? Honey! Come in now. Where are you, Ziggy?"

"Will you be okay?" Ziggy asked me.

"Yeah," I said. "I'll be fine. I'll wait for it to let up a little and then I'll head home."

"Okay," said Ziggy. "June Bug?"

"Yes?"

"I just wanted to say thank you. Thank you for being here today."

"You're welcome," I said.

Ziggy fished Matthew from under the leaves. He walked over to the other side of the hole and hoisted himself through the opening and into the ninth dimension, where the rain was still splashing over the stones. I could hear him scrambling up the hill. Soon Nana Jean would find a warm towel. She would dry his hair and make him chicken soup.

I grabbed Backpack and climbed back out of Majestica and into the ninth dimension.

I let the rain come down on my face and my hair.

Sometimes they love you, but they don't know how to make it stick.

That sounded like it might be true.

But one thing was for sure: Mother wouldn't even be able to try to make it stick if I was covered in mud.

I unzipped Backpack and began taking out the Necessaries one by one. I dabbed rubbing alcohol across my lips. I dipped the toothbrush in mouth-wash. Just a touch. Just enough to smell the scent. I brushed my teeth and under my fingernails in the rain. I found Carrot Scraper and feathered him lightly, lightly across my armpits, down the sides of my neck. Then I took Letter Opener out of Backpack's mouth. The rain made his blade shine.

I held Letter Opener in the air so that his blade was glazed with rain.

Then I rubbed my skin against his smooth, hard surface, first my forehead, then my cheeks, then the bridge of my nose and my chin, then down my neck, down my arms, and down each of my legs.

The blade was smooth and cool. He took away all the disgustingness. The rain fell hard and I was soaked, but I knew I was clean enough for Mother. I left Majestica behind me, a beautiful secret tucked away in the woods, getting farther away as I scrambled up the hill with Backpack on my shoul-ders, back through the boxwoods and the orchard and the garden, and then around the house and onto Trowbridge Road, where rain made puddles on the pavement. I walked across the street and one, two, three houses down to number twenty-eight, where the curtains were drawn and I knew, the way you know that the sun will rise the next day, that once I closed the door behind me, the scent of rain and earth would only be a memory.

I slipped out of my sandals and left Backpack against the porch wall near the door.

I put my hand on the doorknob and opened the door.

I had to push hard. Everything swelled in the rain.

Mother was standing on the front stairs waiting for me. She was leaning against the white wall, one bare foot on a stair, the other wandering forward in space, as though she had thought about descending, but the foot had forgotten what feet do, and so she remained a prisoner of her step, one foot planted, the other unsure. She was wearing a white lace nightgown that made her face look even more drawn and ghostly as she gazed down at me.

"Oh, June Bug," she said. "Oh, June Bug, I'm so glad you're back. You're late."

My heart stopped. "I know," I said. "I'm sorry."

"It's raining. Did you get stuck in the rain?"

I nodded.

"You're all wet."

I imagined what she would do if she were well.

If she were well, she would have taken one look at me and hurried up to the bathroom to get me a towel. She would have wrapped me in it, all fluffy and dry. And then she would have taken me up to my very own bedroom and found some dry clothes in my very own dresser drawers and laid them out on my very own bed for me, and when I was finished changing, she would have come back with a second towel and she would have towel-dried my hair.

There, she would have said. *That's better.*

We looked at each other for a long time. My hair dripped onto the floor.

"I'm going up to change my clothes," I said.

"Okay," said Mother.

But she didn't move up or down the stairs so I had to scooch past her on my way to our bedroom, where I had one drawer in the dresser we shared.

As I passed, Mother snatched my arm and took a long, deep breath through her nose. Mother sniffed my fingers. She sniffed my hand. And then she smiled a tired smile.

"You're clean," she said, with relief.

"Yes," I said. "I am."

"Thank you," said Mother, her voice barely a whisper.

That night I fell asleep with Mother nestled behind me. I had a dream that I was in Majestica, snuggled up in the quilt I used to love best when I had my own room, the pink one with lace along the edge, the one I used to hold up to my face to breathe the scent of sleepiness before closing my eyes and slipping into darkness. I dreamed that Daddy was saying good night to me, the way he used to do before we knew there was such a thing as AIDS. He was wearing the patchwork coat, standing by the bed, and outlined by the silvery light of the full moon, looking down at me with eyes full of love. He put out his hand to touch me, and I stretched my fingertips as far as I could toward him. The air warmed in the space where we almost touched.

What the Cat Dragged In

The next morning, we woke to the sound of someone knocking on our front door.

"Angela? June Bug? You guys up?"

Mother groaned and put the pillow over her head.

I jumped up like a jack-in-the-box. "That's Uncle Toby!" I said happily.

"Tell him to go away," said Mother.

"Hey!" he called again. "I brought you some donuts!"

"It's not even Saturday," Mother muttered. "June, tell him we don't need him."

He knocked again, even louder.

"Hey, Angela. It's raining out here. Would you let me in? I'm getting soaked."

"I don't want him tracking all that rain and dirt into the house. Tell him to go away."

"I don't want him to go away," I said, swinging my legs out of bed. "I'm letting him in."

"Don't you dare," said Mother.

But I was already bouncing out of bed. I flew down the stairs and ran headlong to the heavy wooden door. I grabbed the brass doorknob with both hands and yanked it as hard as I could.

Uncle Toby was drenched. There was rain dripping from his nose. His hair and his beard were soaked. He looked like a cat that someone had left out in a storm.

"Oh my gosh!" I cried. "Oh my gosh, I'm so sorry. Come in! Come in! Hurry!"

He was carrying a soggy bag of donuts and a large brown paper cup of warm coffee that he handed to me. The wonderful smell filled our house, warm and sweet, while the rain lashed against the windows.

"Let's get your mom," he said, and began walking toward the stairs.

I stood in front of him so he couldn't get by.

"You're wet," I said.

"This is true," Uncle Toby said. "You have inherited your father's amazing powers of observation."

"You need to take off your shoes so you don't track mud and stuff into the house."

Uncle Toby untied the laces of his waterlogged work boots. His socks were drenched too. When he took a step, his toes left a semicircle of water on the wooden floor.

My heart froze. "Oh no," I said.

"What?" said Uncle Toby.

"The water. The water on your sock."

"It's just a little rain," whispered Uncle Toby. "I'll clean it up."

"It's not that easy."

"Why not?"

"Because whatever we clean it *with* will need to be cleaned. And then *that* thing will need to be cleaned. And it's not even *Saturday*."

"What's that supposed to mean?"

"Saturday is when we *do* it."

"June Bug," said Uncle Toby. "Please. You aren't

making sense. Listen. Why don't you get me a towel. I'll dry my feet and towel off my head, and I promise, sweetheart, I won't track rain in or mud or anything. Okay? How does that sound?"

"I don't know," I whispered, my voice catching in my throat. "It sounds good in one way, but not good in another."

"Because of the donuts?"

"No."

"Because of the towel?"

I nodded, tears suddenly coming to my eyes. "Yes," I whispered.

"Because you'll have to clean the towel, and then you'll have to clean whatever cleans the towel?"

I nodded again.

Uncle Toby put his hands on either side of my face and kissed my forehead.

"What if I take the towel home?" he whispered.

"You want to take our towel?"

"No," said Uncle Toby, laughing. "I don't want to take your towel. I don't want to take anything from you. All I want is to give you and your mom a donut for breakfast and know that you ate something, and then I want to come back in a couple days and bring you something else. So why don't you go get me a towel. I'll dry myself off. And then we will give this a try. I want to get your mom eating, okay?"

"Okay," I whispered.

I set the coffee and the donuts down by the hallway steps. Then I ran to the kitchen and found an old orange and green hand towel and ran back to Uncle Toby with it. I could still smell the wonderful donuts, warm and sweet, the scent curling up from the bag and filling the room. My stomach trembled.

Uncle Toby took the towel and dried off his feet. Then he dried his hair and beard and then his hands. He tugged open the back door and threw the wet towel onto the porch.

"I'll take that with me when I go. Come on. Let's bring a donut and coffee up to your mom. I haven't been in those upstairs rooms for a long time and I kind of miss them. You think my old bedroom's still there?"

He started walking to the stairs again with the coffee in one hand and the donuts in the other.

"June Bug!" called Mother as soon as his foot touched the first stair. "Tell him *no!*"

I hesitated.

"Tell him no! Tell him no!"

"She doesn't want you to go up there," I said.

"Why not?"

"Because . . ." I began, looking up the stairs toward our bedroom. "Because . . ."

But I didn't know how to finish my sentence because I didn't have the right words. I fell to my knees at the edge of the stairs. I started to cry. I put my hands in front of my mouth so Mother wouldn't hear.

"Oh, honey," muttered Uncle Toby, taking his foot off the stairs and kneeling down on the floor along with me. "Oh, sweetheart. Please. I was only trying to help. I won't go up. I won't go up, I promise." He put his arms around me, and I rested my head in the warm space between his shoulder and his chin, and he rocked me. I could feel his beard on my forehead. He smelled like a woodstove. I closed my eyes against him and I breathed and I breathed, and I tried to gather myself back together.

"How about if you bring a donut up to her? I'll stay down here. Would that be okay?"

"June Bug!" Mother screamed from upstairs. "Tell him it's time to go!"

"I'll bring them after you go," I whispered. "I'm

sorry, Uncle Toby. She's just not feeling that good this morning. She has a stomachache. I think it's the flu. All this rain maybe."

"June!" screeched Mother. Her voice sounded broken.

"You should go," I said. "We'll be okay."

"There's a frosted one in there for you," said Uncle Toby, handing the bag to me. "I know you like them frosted. And there is a plain one for your mom. I picked them out. I was thinking about what you both would like, and I picked them out special."

"Thank you for doing that," I whispered. "Mother and I will eat them together for breakfast. I promise. And I'll give her the coffee. She'll love it."

"Are you sure you don't want me to go up there?" He put his hands on either side of my face and looked into my eyes as though he wanted to find some kind of answer there.

"I'm sure," I said. "I'll bring it to her after you go. It'll be fine. Mother loves donuts and coffee. It will be the perfect thing for her. As soon as she's feeling better. Thank you for coming over, Uncle Toby."

He reached over and pulled his socks and boots back on.

He tied his laces in silence.

"I'm coming back in two days," he said.

"Okay," I whispered.

"I want to try this again."

"Okay."

"I love you more than anything in this whole entire world. Do you know that?"

"I know," I whispered. "I love you too."

When he left, I kept my back turned because I couldn't bear to see him go. I heard him linger in the hallway behind me, maybe looking at me or up the stairs to where he knew my mother was hiding. I heard the sound of the old wooden door opening, and then the sound of the rain and the door closing softly behind me, and then the clattering sound of Uncle Toby's truck pulling back onto Trowbridge Road and out in the rain toward town.

I wiped tears from my cheeks. I took a deep, shaking breath in and then out. I carried the donuts and the coffee into the kitchen and put them on the table. I took out two plates and two forks and two knives and set the table all nice and pretty. I put a donut on each plate. The plain one and the frosted one. I put the coffee down next to the plain donut and sat down across from it. *Want a donut, darling? I picked them out especially for you. Try them. Try them.*

They are sweet and delicious. "Thank you," I said out loud in the empty kitchen. "Don't mind if I do." I took my knife and my fork, and I ate my frosted donut one tiny bite at a time, so that maybe, just maybe, I could convince myself for a little bit longer that there are some kinds of sweetnesses that really do last forever.

Beasts from the Shadows

The path to Majestica was transformed by rain. Mushrooms emerged from the ground with warm, wet lips. Some poked blindly beneath the leaves like the heads of sleeping turtles. Some unfurled like white feathers from the damp bark of the hollow logs. Others gathered in choirs to sing quiet blessings to each other, their golden heads bowed and their eyes closed tight. The sun shone on our heads. We sat cross-legged in the leaves and watched everything sparkle. Ziggy took off Jenny's necklace and held it up to the sun, and the beads gleamed red and orange and purple like tiny flames. He tucked it behind his ear. Matthew scrambled from Ziggy's shoulder, found a tiny brown toad the size of a pebble, and pounced around the leaves after it.

The two creatures danced together. They scrambled around the forest floor, the sound of unseen creatures rustling beneath the leaves. I wondered what other invisible beasts might be hiding nearby without our ever realizing it, buried in pine needles or gazing at us from treetops. Matthew emerged with the toad in his jaws, his tail bristling with pride. He lifted his white face, chewed twice, and swallowed.

I stood up and took a deep breath. The ninth dimension smelled like wet leaves and dandelions. Up toward Nana Jean's orchard, the peaches and apples were getting so heavy that the trees bowed their heads.

I lifted my face and called, "Come out, come out, wherever you are!" so that every invisible beast could hear me.

Slowly, creatures that had been hiding emerged from the shadows like details in a hidden-object picture, the bark of the trees wrinkling, the branches shifting until they were all around us: beasts from the shadows, the color of earth.

The first to emerge was the bark beast. She stepped from the tree with her long, craggy face and wrinkled brown wings. She shook herself free, sniffed the air, and began making a strange, low, grumbling howl of freedom.

Then came the leaf beast, who flicked herself up from a leaf pile with her pointy face and paper-thin claws. She tumbled her papery body toward me, winking as a sign of ancient respect, and then whisked and twirled away, taken by the wind.

The stone wall shivered.

Three bald, round-backed stone beasts the size of potatoes rolled from their crumbled piles like petrified babies and blinked at us with gray impassive eyes.

There were leagues of pinecone and pine needle and acorn and pebble and mushroom beasts, popping from the ground to wander about in hordes, so many that we had to be careful not to step on them, and they had to be careful not to bump into one another with their tiny heads.

Last of all, as though performing a grand finale, the biggest hollow log rolled onto her side and became a magnificent hollow log beast, with her long, broad body and wise snuffling face. She lumbered over to us, grunting joyously.

"Welcome, beast," I said to her softly. And then I raised my face. "Welcome, all of you."

The bark beast barked.

The acorn beast chirped.

The ninth dimension was filled with the rumble and buzz of creatures thanking me for bringing them to life.

The hollow log beast took a very deep breath and blew a long, low howl.

Matthew scrambled onto Ziggy's head. He was shivering.

"It's okay, Matthew," said Ziggy.

Matthew ducked under Ziggy's hair.

"Come, beasts," I called. "Come, beautiful beasts. Come dance with us!"

We led them all around the ninth dimension, the stone and the pebble beasts, the pinecone and the pine needle beasts, the acorn and the mushroom beasts, the bark, the leaf, and the hollow log beast— all twirling and tripping and galumphing after us in an enormous conga line.

We drummed on the ground.

We stomped.

We howled and buzzed and grunted and snorted and grumbled. We twirled in a massive stomping crowd, stone beasts with acorn beasts, bark beast with leaf beast, and me and Ziggy in the middle, stomping our bare feet and howling louder than any of them.

But then there was a horrible sound that didn't fit at all.

Cruel laughter.

Buzz Crowley was standing on the top of the hill and sneering at us in disgust.

"Well, would you look at this. It's the crazy girl and the fairy boy."

The hollow log beast sighed and turned back into a hollow log.

The bark beast stepped back into the tree.

The stone beasts faded back into the old stone wall.

We stopped dancing. I reached out and took Ziggy's hand.

"Looks like the two neighborhood freaks have finally found each other."

John-John laughed as though what Buzz just said was the funniest thing he ever heard in his life. The horrible sound spread through the ninth dimension like a plague.

"Get out," said Ziggy. "You're not wanted here."

"Oh, we're not?" said Buzz. "What are you going to do about it? This is public land. *Anyone* can play here. It's not like we're trespassing or something."

"You *are* trespassing," I said. "And for your information, this is *my* land. It has always *been* my land, and I want you *out* of here right *now* or you'll be *sorry!*"

Buzz narrowed his eyes. "Are you challenging me?" he asked. He picked up a big stick.

John-John picked up a big stick too.

"Yes," I said. "I'm challenging you."

"Okay," said Buzz. "You asked for it."

The brothers looked at each other and nodded. Then Buzz and John-John came running down the hill with their sticks.

Ziggy picked up a stray stone beast and ran toward them, screaming.

He threw the stone beast at Buzz's head.

He missed.

Buzz grabbed Ziggy by the shoulders and shoved

him onto the ground. He put the heel of his foot on Ziggy's back.

"Get off!" screamed Ziggy. "Get off of me!"

John-John held up his stick. "I'm gonna whack him," he said.

"No!"

Ziggy covered his face.

Buzz used his foot to push Ziggy's face hard into the leaves. He moved his foot back and forth so Ziggy's face smeared against the ground. Ziggy struggled to get up, but Buzz kept kicking him back down.

"Stop it," I said.

"Why should I?" said Buzz.

"Yeah," said John-John. "Why should he?"

I thought about what to do for a moment. They were too big for me to fight. They were too mean for me to plead with. But they were stupid. And they were cruel. Maybe I could use that to trick them somehow.

"Because if you don't," I said, making my voice hateful like theirs, "I'm going to give you AIDS."

"That's dumb," said Buzz.

I took a step closer.

"Didn't you hear what Lucy Delmato said? My

daddy died of AIDS and everyone in my house has it. If I give it to you, you'll die of it too. Do you want that?"

My own words nauseated me.

Buzz laughed and poked the stick into Ziggy's hair. He found Jenny's beads with the tip of the stick and flung them deep into the woods. Then he ran the stick up and down Ziggy's back and poked him with it in the butt.

"You like that?" he said. "You like that, you little fairy?"

"No," said Ziggy, muffled into the leaves. "I don't like that at all."

John-John put his stick on Ziggy's butt too.

I spit on the ground. "That spit has AIDS in it," I told them.

"My teacher says you can't get AIDS from spit," said John-John.

"You can if there's enough of it. Also, I have a canker sore in my mouth and it's bleeding. I'm going to kiss you with my canker sore, and you're going to die from AIDS." I puckered up and took a step forward. "Come over here."

Buzz and John-John both took a step backward.

Ziggy pulled himself out of the leaves. His

face was smeared with dirt and tears. He stood there blinking and breathing hard. His hands were clenched into fists.

"What are you looking at?" Buzz said to Ziggy. "You want to kiss me too?"

"What's that?" said Ziggy.

"He does," said John-John. "He loves you. He wants to kiss you."

I charged at John-John. I juiced up and spit a big, wet loogie right in his eye.

"There's blood in there," I said in a low voice. "Now you're gonna die."

John-John screamed and dropped his stick. He started wiping his eye furiously.

"Don't be such a wuss," Buzz told him, but he looked uncertain, and when John-John leaned into him and whispered, "I don't want to die," Buzz dropped his stick and put his arm around his brother's shoulder.

"You're not gonna die," he whispered back. "We'll get you to a doctor."

"It's too late," I said. "Once you've been infected with AIDS, you have it forever. There's no cure. Kiss me, Buzz," I said, coming closer. I picked up the stick and made myself smile a huge, crazy, cross-eyed smile. "Kiss me right on the canker sore." I licked my lips and drooled and spit and charged at him, still grinning my crazy-girl grin and puckering and spitting the whole way. "You're gonna die of AIDS, just like John-John and my daddy. You're gonna *die*, Buzz Crowley. They're gonna bury you, and the maggots will eat out your eyes. Kiss me."

The two boys took one more look at my wet, slurpy face, and one more look at each other, and then, without even talking about it, they hightailed it out of there and ran like their pants were on fire, falling down and picking themselves up, and climbing over each other and screaming all the way up the hill and back around the house to Trowbridge Road.

I knelt down in the leaves with the stick in my hand and I sobbed, my own hateful, lying, horrible words echoing all around me.

Ziggy sat down beside me. His face was smeared with dirt.

"You were brave," he said.

"I wasn't," I muttered.

"You stood up for me," said Ziggy. "No one has ever done that before."

"My daddy would have been ashamed of me. He

would have hated to hear me talking about AIDS that way. Using fear to make them run away."

"I think he would have been proud," said Ziggy. "At school one time I tried to fight some bullies. I scratched a boy in the face so hard, he had to go to the hospital for stitches. We were both suspended. And then when I got back, the fighting got worse. You figured out a way to make them stop that didn't hurt anyone."

"You're wrong," I whispered. "It did hurt."

Matthew appeared out of nowhere and danced at our feet, chirring and trying to make us smile, which we might have done if we had not been sobbing. I scratched the top of Matthew's head.

The beasts stayed in the shadows and watched me cry. They didn't know what tears were. This was the first time they had seen meanness, and to them, death was just the end of a day, no more sad than a sunset. They didn't come out, but I could feel their eyes on me while I cried, my body shuddering. Ziggy put his arm around my shoulders, his head leaning against my head. The beasts watched while Ziggy walked into the woods to find Jenny's beads. They watched while I fumbled around for Backpack, where I would find the Necessaries I needed to erase the disgustingness and lies.

I poured a capful of mouthwash into my mouth. I gargled hard, sloshing it over my tongue and over my teeth. I spit a stream of mouthwash into the leaves and then spit again and again and again until there was nothing left.

Masks

———◆———

Uncle Toby came back two days later, just like he said he would.

I sat at the table in my pajamas while he took things out of a paper bag and put them on the counter. There was butter, a pear, a loaf of Wonder Bread, and a hunk of salami. Just enough.

"I'm heading to the Highlands this afternoon to check out that apartment I told you about," he said. "If it's halfway decent and I can afford the rent, I'll sign the agreement and pay the deposit, and then I can move in at the end of the month."

"I hope you can afford it," I said.

"Me too," said Uncle Toby.

He took out the salami and cut it into thin slices. Then he found a frying pan, lit the stove, dropped in the butter, and started to fry the salami. It hissed and spattered in the pan. There is nothing in this world that smells better when you're hungry than salami fried in butter. Some people say God's gift to breakfast is bacon. But they have never smelled salami spattering in the pan or heard the sound of salami slices turning themselves into little round cups, the edges curling up, dark and crispy.

I had not yet eaten my first piece when Mother's voice came tight and broken from our room upstairs. "Are you finished down there?"

The scent of the fried salami curled up the stairs, beckoning her with its savory tendrils.

"Toby?" Mother called down in her bedclothes. Her voice sounded happy, but it was a mask, as though she were trying to hide her panic from him and from all the germs floating around the kitchen below her, the disgustingness from Uncle Toby's fingers, from the soles of his boots. "Toby? Hi down there. It is so nice of you to drop in again, but I think

June Bug is done eating. Thanks so much for stopping by. See you soon!"

"I haven't even started!" I screamed up to her.

I was surprised at the venom in my voice. It didn't sound like me. But it felt good.

Uncle Toby met my eyes.

"Why don't you come down," Toby called up the stairs. "This is good stuff, Angela. Wouldn't hurt you to get some meat on your bones, either."

"You're so sweet, but no thank you," Mother called. "So, bye. See you next time."

"If you don't come down, I'll bring a plate up to you. Angela, Marty made me promise I would look after things around here. I've barely seen your face since the funeral. You're always up there, hiding in your room."

Uncle Toby put a piece of fried salami on a plate along with a piece of Wonder Bread and a slice of pear. He pushed his chair away from the table. "I'm on my way upstairs. I've got some food for you."

"I'm just not very hungry this morning. Another time, okay?" Her voice cracked from upstairs, the sweetness giving way to desperation.

"No," said Uncle Toby. "I want to take a look at you."

I clutched the edge of the table.

Uncle Toby began walking toward the stairs.

"No!" screamed Mother from her room.

He froze in midstep.

"Please don't!" she screamed again. "Please?" and then softer, now that she could tell the footsteps weren't continuing. "Please. I'll come down. Okay? I'll come down to you. Just, please. Go back to the table. Just go back and sit down with June. I'll have something to eat. I promise. Just don't come up. You can't come up here."

Hearing her voice with Uncle Toby in the house changed everything.

When I was alone with her, it was easier to pretend that things made sense. But with Uncle Toby in the kitchen, cringing every time she spoke, I found myself suddenly off balance. It was as though I had been walking on a rope bridge a hundred feet up. The bridge swayed back and forth over a raging river, but I had been keeping myself steady by pretending the bridge was strong. Suddenly there was another person with me. He saw things the way they really were. When he told me to look down and watch my step, I suddenly I saw that the bridge was made of frayed rope, and with every step I swayed from a dizzying height. That raging water I thought was lovely would actually kill me if I missed a step.

Uncle Toby backed up to the table with Mother's plate in his hands.

"Are you sitting down?"

He sat.

"Yes, Angela," he said. "I'm sitting down."

"Okay," she said, her voice small and uncertain. "I'm coming down the stairs. Stay there, please. And don't get up to hug me or kiss my cheek or anything."

"I wouldn't dream of it," said Toby.

We could hear her footsteps coming. Small and light as a child's.

Now Uncle Toby would see her face.

The same face I saw every day of my life.

But suddenly I was wondering if I had ever really seen it.

Even once we knew the time was coming for Daddy to leave us—even after we moved him downstairs into the dining room so that he could look out the window at the birds—Mother stopped me from getting close enough to see how his face was changing. I could never really get a good look at the way his eyes were sinking into their sockets, the way his hair that had always been long and thick had become fragile and soft.

Mother emerged in the stairwell and froze there, poised in the threshold. One white hand clutched the banister, and the other held the wall. She composed herself to smile at us, the muscles in her face so unused to performing the necessary tasks that it seemed more like a grimace than a smile. I realized how much she had changed since the funeral, as though she had been the one in the final stages of illness, the bones in her face, in her wrists protruding, her skin ashen against the starched white of her nightgown.

"Oh, Angela," said Uncle Toby. He rose to his feet.

"No!" snapped Mother. And then when it was clear he was not going to move toward her, more gently, "No, Toby. Please sit down. This isn't as bad as it looks. I'm fine. Really. I just haven't had much of an appetite since Marty passed away."

"Angela," said Toby. "This isn't good."

Mother made herself smile again, but it was as if she were following step-by-step instructions for smiling without having to feel any actual joy.

"I think you need some help, Angela. I think you need to see someone."

Mother leaned back against the banister. She tipped her head so that it was lolling against the wall behind her. "You are such a good brother-in-law. Marty would be thankful, I'm sure. But we don't need any help. We're fine, me and June Bug. Here. Look. I'm hungry today. I think I'll eat a sandwich. June Bug, sweetheart? Be a dear and make Mother a delicious salami sandwich. It smells so good, I can't help myself."

I stared at her, not quite sure what to do.

"I'll make it," said Uncle Toby reaching for the bread.

"Stop!" Mother snapped before his hand could touch it. And then more gently, when he put his hand back in his lap, "No need to trouble yourself. June Bug can do it. Okay, sweetheart? And then you bring it over here to Mommy nice and careful."

My hands fumbled and shook. I tried as hard as I could not to touch too much. I got four pieces of salami on the bread with a fork. I picked the sandwich up with a napkin. I turned my face to the side so that I didn't breathe on it.

Uncle Toby watched me cross the kitchen with the fried salami sandwich held ceremoniously in front of me.

"Oh, thank you so much, honey," said Mother in her strange, tight voice. She reached out and gave me a brief hug. And then she took the sandwich from me. She held the bread in her hands. She sniffed at it, miserably.

I backed up to the table and sat down.

Uncle Toby watched her.

The room was silent.

"You gonna eat it?" I snapped.

My voice was a fist.

"Of course, I am going to eat it, June Bug. I'm just enjoying how good it smells first."

"Stop sniffing at it and chew," I said, surprised again at the venom in my voice.

"June Bug, so help me," Mother threatened, her eyes smoldering.

"You need my help? Okay. I'm helping you."

Uncle Toby put his hand on my shoulder to steady me. "Angela, let's not play games here. If you can't eat, you need help. That's all there is to it.

Either you eat and I leave here, or you don't and we head over to the hospital. What's it going to be?"

Mother stared at Uncle Toby. She put the sandwich to her lips. She paused a moment. Then she took a bite. She chewed and swallowed.

"Delicious," she said through gritted teeth.

"Great," I said. "Now finish it."

Mother took more bites. We watched her pretend to like it.

It was not a very convincing performance.

"Aren't you going to eat the crust?" I asked her.

Her eyes burned holes into my face.

But she ate the crust. Expressionless.

She never took her eyes off me the entire time.

"Thank you," said Toby. "At least I know you had one meal today."

"Toby," said Mother quietly, "please go now."

"I'm not sure I'm ready to go," said Uncle Toby. "I want to think a minute."

"You told me that if I ate the sandwich, you would go. I've eaten it. I kept my side of the bargain. Now, please. I'm tired. I'm upset. I need to talk to my daughter. It's time for you to go home now."

Uncle Toby ran a hand through his hair. He looked uncertain.

"It's okay, Uncle Toby," I said, softly. "You can go. We'll be fine."

"Are you sure?"

Mother and I stared at each other.

The air crackled between us.

"Yes," I said, keeping my eyes on Mother's face. "Yes, I'm sure. I'll see you soon. Thanks for coming over. Good luck with the apartment."

Uncle Toby reached out and took my chin, moving my face so that I would look at him.

"I'll be back tomorrow," he told me. And then toward my mother. "You hear me, Angela? I'm coming back tomorrow, and you're going to have more to eat." Then he grasped me and kissed my forehead. "You call me if you need me before then, okay? You call me anytime."

"I will," I said, trying to make myself sound confident.

"Toby," said Mother, cringing. *"Please."*

"All right," he said. "All right, I'm going. I'll be back tomorrow. Be good to each other. Okay? Don't do anything crazy."

Neither of us said anything. We watched each other's faces while the screen door slammed. Then there was the familiar sound of the engine of his truck turning over and he switched on the radio before backing out of our driveway. We could hear the sound of rock and roll as he headed off down Trowbridge Road, getting softer now, the sound waves bending as he turned the corner from Trowbridge and back into Newton Highlands.

We stood in the kitchen in silence.

We stared at each other, our fury sizzling around us like static electricity.

"We need to talk about what just happened," Mother said.

"What do you want to talk about?"

"What you just did to me in front of Uncle Toby was very rude."

"I encouraged you to eat a sandwich," I said. "Why was that rude?"

"It was blackmail. Toby was going to have me taken away."

I shrugged.

"You don't care? You know what would happen to you if someone took me away?"

I shrugged again. But inside, my stomach was twisted in knots.

"You will end up in some institution. Or a foster home. Is that what you want, June?"

"Yes," I said. "That's what I want."

"You don't mean that," Mother said.

"I do," I say. "Anything would be better than living here with you."

Mother opened her mouth but did not speak.

"I'm going out now," I told her.

"No," she whispered. "You're staying here."

I turned my back on her.

"Stay here, June Bug! Don't you dare leave me!"

I marched out of the kitchen, down the front hallway, and onto the porch.

Backpack was waiting for me.

"June Bug!" Mother screeched from inside.

But her voice already seemed far away.

Kitchen Songs

I marched down Trowbridge Road, my shuttered house shrinking behind me like a tomb with Mother trapped inside.

Backpack clattered on my back.

I liked the feeling of straps on my shoulders, the weight reminding me that I had muscles. Even if someone put out their foot and tried to trip me, even if they pushed my back with two hands the way Lucy Delmato pushed me once on the swings, I could steady myself. I was strong. A soldier knows how to keep on marching. I was not at all like

Mother. I was a different kind of creature entirely. I was a nomad of the ninth dimension. I had powers beyond belief. I could punch a hole through the clouds with my power.

When I got close to Nana Jean's house, I could see her standing on the steps watching me, smiling and holding out her arms.

I approached her slowly and stopped in front of her, uncertain of what to do. Her body settled in front of mine, her arms extended.

"Well," she said, "are you going to just stand there, or are you going to give Nana Jean a hug?"

As soon as it became clear that I was not going to move on my own, she went ahead and pulled me close, pressing my cheek into the round buttons of her housedress. All at once she was hugging me hard.

It was a rocking, rollicking, gorgeous hug that melted me from the inside and made me want to be cradled like a baby, made me want her to brush my hair and dress me and feed me and sing me lullabies.

"Well, that's better," said Nana Jean. "I always think a hug is the best way to turn a day around. Don't you? Ziggy told me that you've become friends. He said you might like to have some lunch with us. You hungry?"

I nodded.

"Well, come inside. There's plenty."

I took a tentative step forward.

"Look at you," Nana Jean said. "You must be starving."

"I am," I said.

"Well, let's go, then. Come with me."

Nana Jean took my hand and led me inside her house.

I had waved hello, walking down the street. I had been in the tree hundreds of times. I had even been on her porch for trick-or-treating. But never in my entire life had I ever been inside Nana Jean's house. The front hallway was lined with bookshelves full of old, dusty books. There was a carved wooden banister that curved up the winding stairs, promising more unseen rooms where people walked and slept and lived, maybe with their windows and doors wide open. I couldn't help closing my eyes and taking a long breath through my nose. I knew what that smell was. It was freedom. Nana Jean stroked my hand.

"Don't cry, honey. Everything is going to be okay."

I hadn't realized I was crying.

I wiped my eyes with the back of my arm.

Nana Jean led me into the kitchen.

Ziggy and Matthew were at the table already.

Ziggy had a napkin tucked into the front of his shirt. He was holding a knife and fork.

"Hello, June Bug Jordan," Ziggy said.

"Hi," I said, still grasping Nana Jean's hand.

"I decided you needed one of Nana Jean's home-cooked meals. Is that okay?"

I nodded.

"Sit down, honey," said Nana Jean. "We've already set a place for you. You know when your daddy and Uncle Toby were little boys and your grandma was working, they used to come over to play with my Jenny, and I cooked them lunch here plenty of times. Your daddy would sit right there in that same seat you're sitting in. You look a lot like him, you know that?"

I nodded.

It felt good to hear those words coming from her.

The inside of Nana Jean's kitchen was just how I always imagined it would be: filled with the ghosts of tantalizing meals. Generations of lasagna. Leagues of Italian wedding soup.

Nana Jean's kitchen smelled like the gossip of garlic and bacon and oregano. It smelled like the laughter of sun-dried tomatoes and sausages and cheese. The recipes whispered to each other from the glazed windows to the spaces between the floorboards to the countertops. *We have fed the children and grandchildren in here. We meals. We blessed, blessed meals.* I entered like Alice on the threshold of Wonderland, or Dorothy taking her first steps into the Emerald City—the prickling feeling that I was about to enter something glorious.

She did not ask me what I wanted to eat. How could I be expected to answer such a question? My desire to be filled was boundless. I might as well have answered that I wanted to swallow both of them, and the ferret and the tree and the kitchen and the whole neighborhood, but even after devouring all of this, I still would not be satisfied.

I was grateful when Nana Jean began bringing food to the table anyway. She presented us with a feast as if we were royalty.

This is not the kind of food Mother helped me prepare at our house, food we could cook without tasting or touching. Soup from cans. Cold cuts from white wax paper. These were recipes that Nana Jean's hands needed to touch. They required stirring and chopping, required her fingers to feel the brush of egg white, the grain of table salt—maybe even for her tongue to taste something uncooked, just a tiny piece, to tell if the spices were right. How can you cook without tasting? You need to imagine the other person's tongue to know if everything is perfect.

Nana Jean sat with us.

She did not try to talk to us. She leaned forward, sometimes nodding when we swallowed, as though eating was a kind of conversation. *Do you love it?* asked the plate. We answered by lifting the fork to our lips again. *Yes,* our bellies whispered. *We love it.*

A Choir of Crows

———◆———

After lunch, Nana Jean went upstairs to take a nap.

Ziggy grabbed a quilt and an embroidered pillow from the rocking chair by the woodstove. He draped the quilt over my shoulders. "For Majestica," he said.

Then he put Matthew on his head, tucked the pillow under his arm, and led me back through the kitchen, out the back door, and into the garden. The sun was shining, and everything was lush and green. The tomatoes were so juicy, they looked like they were going to explode, and the leafy tops of carrots sprang like green fireworks from the ground. I held the quilt around my shoulders, and together we dodged through the apple and peach orchard, past the boxwoods, and down the hill into the ninth dimension, with the quilt dragging behind us, picking up twigs and leaves. Today the ground was spattered with dandelions, yellow and gleaming as though the sun had licked its tongue across the ground.

"It's even more beautiful than it was yesterday," I whispered.

"Of course," Ziggy said. "Everything's more beautiful when you're full."

"How did you know I was hungry?"

Ziggy looked at me. His eyes were sad and serious.

"When you put your arms up to climb the tree, I could see your ribs."

"You're skinny too, you know."

"I know," said Ziggy. "That's why I noticed."

Ziggy dropped the embroidered pillow on the ground. Then he raised his shirt.

"I've gained some weight since I moved in with Nana Jean," he said.

"Didn't Jenny feed you?" I asked.

Ziggy hesitated before speaking.

"Sometimes," he said.

"Only sometimes?"

"When she drinks, she forgets."

We looked at each other.

"Want to see something else?" he asked.

"Yes," I whispered, suddenly a little scared of what he was going to show me next.

Ziggy turned his arm so his wrist was facing up. There was a scar, the shape of a crescent moon.

"Where did you get that?" I ask.

"Cigarette lighter."

I touched the scar. It was silky and smooth.

"Do you like it?" he asked me.

"No," I said. "I don't. Not at all."

"Neither do I," said Ziggy. "But it's nothing compared to what he does to Jenny."

"What who does?"

"Donny," said Ziggy.

"It's a good thing we have Majestica," I said. "Now there's always somewhere we can go if things get really bad."

"It will always be here for us," said Ziggy.

"Let's look for talismans for spells of safety, and then we'll bring down the pillow and blanket."

We dropped the bedding and Backpack and Matthew in the dandelions and set off to look for treasure. We searched among the leaves, digging around by the stone pile and the hollow log. Ziggy found the handle of a cracked water jug, a railroad nail, and the black leather sole of an old boot.

I found a clay marble, a piece of petrified coal, and a bunch of old glass bottles in various states of disrepair. Ziggy found a Coca-Cola bottle filled with moss and a tiny blue medicine bottle. We wrapped all our treasures in the quilt, scooped up the pillow, and brought it all down into Majestica, where the sun slanted through the branches.

"It is so beautiful in here," Ziggy said.

"Safe from anyone who can hurt us."

Together, we threw all the sticks and rocks away from the far side so all that was left were leaves. Then we scooped up armfuls of leaves from the near side, piling them into a great heap so that there was more of a cushion for sleeping.

We spread the quilt over the leaf pile and set down the pillow. Then we arranged the treasures in the spaces between the rocks on the walls around us. The sole of the boot. The railroad nail, the tiny blue medicine bottle, the broken water jug handle—all lined up like talismans on a magician's mantelpiece. "Perfect for protection," I said.

"Let's see how it feels to sleep here," said Ziggy.

We lay down on the quilt. Ziggy put the embroidered pillow beneath my head, but I scooched over and made room for him. I took a deep breath through my nose. Majestica smelled like wet stones and earth and leaves. It smelled alive and damp. You could almost believe that just breathing here could make you whole again.

We closed our eyes and pretended that it was our destiny to be here in this cellar hole among the ghosts, the shadowy voices of old milk cows lowing in the distance, the long, deep breaths of a husband and wife who slept here when Trowbridge Road was just a path scarred by wagon wheels.

When we fell asleep, we were the farmer and his wife. We were ninety years old, and this was the old house that we built from the trees we cut down ourselves. This was the farm we worked with our own hands. All our children grew up here. Some of them made it and some of them didn't, the little fallen gravestones tucked away under the leaves somewhere.

This was where we took care of each other when

there was illness, fetching water from the pump, a pyramid of birch logs in the fireplace, warming us even when the winters seemed endless and the larder was low, and the farm was filled with crows at dusk, the sound of their feathery voices in the bare January trees echoing everywhere, their bodies, when we ran to the frosted windows to look, like thousands of black leaves.

"I'm going out there," I told the farmer. "I want to be one of them."

I took his hand and we rose from our bed, crossing to the near side with our old legs. We could see the dusky sky through the opening and the bleak shape of winter trees. We climbed up into the winter, a farmer and his wife.

It was January and the farm was covered in snow. The fallow cornfields and the trees surrounding us were filled with screeching crows, black bodies shifting from one branch to another. I spread my arms to either side of me and screeched to tell them I was coming, and then I screeched again until my arms were black wings and my eyes were shining.

I lifted into the sky. Ziggy lifted behind me.

We flapped to the top of a tree to join our

brothers and sisters, every branch covered in the thrumming bodies of our flock. This is when I discovered that what I used to think was screeching was actually singing. We were a chorus of ten thousand crows. We sang about cornfields. We sang about sunsets. We sang about snow.

And then something in the air shifted.

I couldn't describe what it was. The wind, maybe. In unison, we rose from the tree and swirled, singing into the sky over the fallow fields, the tiny farmhouse and the barn and the sheds and the farmer and his wife and the gravestones for the children who didn't make it far below us, and we winged and circled in a wild dance.

But they flew away.

Thousands of them together. Darkening the sky.

Whirling and roiling. Flapping away.

All except a white one, who winked at us with his shining red eye and, instead of flying away, descended to the roof of the barn. We couldn't help it. We were tethered there. We followed him downward toward the farm, and then down from the roof of the barn to the stone wall, and then to the fallow cornfield and the snowy ground, the voices of our brothers and sisters getting fainter and fainter above us as they flew away, a swirling black cloud singing through the sky.

When we landed, it was summertime again.

And we were Ziggy and June standing side by side next to the pile of fieldstones.

When I turned to Ziggy, I could see that he was crying.

I reached over and put my hand on his shoulder. He tried to smile.

We found Matthew curled up in a clump of dandelions.

Ziggy put Matthew on his head, and I swung Backpack onto my shoulder.

I took Ziggy's hand and turned it so his wrist was facing up and I could see the little crescent moon. I touched it with one finger. Then I brought his arm to my face and leaned my cheek against it.

"Thank you," whispered Ziggy.

He headed back up the hill, past the boxwoods, past the orchard, and into Nana Jean's garden, where he disappeared from view.

I knelt by myself in the dandelions.

Majestica was just a cellar hole covered with

branches. I opened Backpack and held my breath. I poured mouthwash into my cupped palm and scrubbed my face, splashing it across my lips, rinsing my hands in it, tipping my head back and gargling. I spit a stream of mouthwash into the leaves.

Sarabande

As soon as I opened the door to our house, I could tell something was wrong. Mother was crouching half-in, half-out of the stairway, as though she had frozen on her way up the stairs. She waited by the railing, twirling her hair with her fingers. When I came near, she covered her face and shrunk back against the wall. The room smelled horrible.

One time a mouse died behind the stove. Daddy said there was nothing to do about the smell but wait until the body dried out. Until then, all we could do was breathe through our mouths and hope it would all be over soon. The first few days were the worst. And then the smell faded. Maybe another mouse had died in our kitchen.

"It's me," Mother said, finally from her dark corner.

She straightened her body so I could see.

"Oh, Mother," I said.

"It was the fried salami," she muttered. "I needed to get it out."

"You made yourself throw up?"

"That salami was infected. Now I have AIDS."

"People don't catch AIDS from salami," I told her.

"How do you know?" Mother whispered, trembling.

"Because it makes no sense."

"That's not a reason. I ate the virus. I put it into my mouth."

"Mother," I said. "Listen to me."

"I should have recognized the signs. The hemorrhoids. The sores. Each slice was filled with them. I tried to get them out. But now it's all over the house."

"Mother."

"Toby's salami did me in. Call hospice. I'm ready to go." She held herself and rocked, miserably.

"Mother, please. Let's get you in the bath. The salami didn't have AIDS. I promise."

"But how do you know?" Her voice trembled.

"Come on," I said. "You'll feel better after a bath."

I reached out for her.

"Don't touch me," she said.

"It's okay. Look. I'll put on latex gloves first."

I found the box of disposables under the sink and snapped them onto my hands. When I touched her again, it was the latex and not my fingertip that slid against her murky sleeve and held her damp hand. I walked first, stopping at every step to make sure she was making her way. One step and then a rest. Another step and then a rest. She grasped my fingers.

I helped her undress.

She sat on the toilet while I ran the bath.

I turned both faucets on full force.

"Only use hot water," she said. "It needs to be scalding to do any good."

I nodded and turned off the cold.

Pretty soon, the air in the bathroom was steamy.

"Are you sure the salami didn't have AIDS?" she asked, shivering on the toilet.

"Yes, Mother."

"How sure are you?"

"99.9999 percent," I said.

"Why not 100 percent? I thought you said you were sure. Any percent except 100 means you have doubts. How sure are you? Completely sure, or not completely sure?"

"Completely sure."

"Put in six caps of Clorox," Mother ordered.

I did.

The scent of bleach swirled in the air.

"So you're sure?"

"Yes," I said again, watching the chemicals dance.

"It is a pretty strange idea, I guess."

I turned to look at her. She was sitting on the toilet trying to smile.

"I think you were just upset," I said.

"I *was* upset," she said.

"Because I was mean to you when Toby came. And then you made yourself throw up."

"Because I thought the salami had AIDS?"

"Right."

"So you would feel sorry for me?"

"Maybe." I touched the water with the underside of my wrist. It was ready.

"Put in another two caps of Clorox."

I did what she said.

Mother stepped one foot and then the other foot into the tub. She lowered herself down, leaned against the back of the tub, and slid into the water up to her chin.

"So, *do* you?" she asked.

"Do I what?"

"Do you feel sorry for me?"

I looked down at my mother's body.

"Yes," I said.

"Good," said Mother. "Because I have been through a lot."

"Yes, Mother." I sighed. "You *have* been through a lot."

"And so have you. You lost both your father *and* your mother."

The bleach twisted and twirled. It made my eyes sting.

"Did you mean it when you said you would rather be in a foster home than here in our house with me?"

"No," I told her. "I didn't mean it."

My words rang like lies.

"Good," said Mother. "Because if you meant that, it would be really horrible."

"Yes," I said. "It would be."

Mother took the bristle brush from its hook on the side of the tub. She started with her arm, scrubbing with quick, hard strokes.

"Why are you looking at me that way?" Mother asked.

"I don't know," I told her. "I'm just tired."

I turned my face away. I could smell the Clorox dancing and hear the sound of water lapping against her skin and the rasp of Mother's breathing as she scrubbed all the germs away.

When it was over, I brought her a clean white nightgown from the hook in the hall and draped it over the edge of the sink. Then I held her elbow as she stepped from the tub, one candlestick leg and then the other.

I used a clean white towel to dry her. I wiped the water from her face. She smiled at me. Serene. Clean. Mother closed her eyes and leaned her face into my hand. Then I climbed on top of the closed toilet and lowered the white gown over her head.

The fresh cotton smelled like morning. It made her look like an angel.

"I feel better," she whispered.

"Good," I said.

"Thank you, June Bug."

I didn't say anything.

"Did you hear me?"

"Yes. I heard you. You said, 'Thank you.'"

"I meant it," Mother said. "I really meant it. I am grateful for you."

"Okay," I said.

"You are the only person in the world who understands me."

I looked at her. She was so fragile, a breath could break her.

Mother took a step toward me. She pulled my head onto her shoulder and stroked my hair. She hugged me, her fingers moving across my back.

"Come on," Mother whispered into my hair. "I want to show you something."

I followed her into our room. She took out her cello and sat down on the stool.

"Did you know which movement was Daddy's favorite?"

"The Prelude?"

"No," Mother said. "He loved the Sarabande best. Because even though the tempo is slow, it always seems to go by too fast. Like a comma, he always said. Or a sigh."

"Or his life."

"Yes." Mother agreed, smiling weakly. "Like his life. Like all of our lives, I guess."

She began to play, drawing her bow across the strings.

The Sarabande is woven with chords and double-stops. It seemed she was playing three parts at once, a triangle of voices. Ghosts singing valentines to each other. I imagined that Daddy was the melody and Mother and I were the bass notes underneath, reaching for him but never quite touching.

Remember me. Remember me. Remember me, his notes pleaded.

How could I forget you? Mother's notes assured him, strong and resonant at the bottom.

I'm sorry I wasn't enough, my notes whispered in the middle, almost unheard, ashamed of what they needed to say. *I was cruel on the day you died. I didn't have the chance to apologize. I love you.*

Sometimes the notes were so close together, they seemed to kiss each other, but then the melody stepped away from the bass notes, moved off down the road on its own. *Goodbye. Goodbye.* Faded into the distance.

Lace and Earth

One in the morning folded into two in the morning, and two in the morning dissolved into three. Back and forth. Back and forth from the stairs to the sink to the stairs to the sink until I felt like I had worn a canyon beneath my feet. But still, my job was far from finished.

Once the walls and stairs were clean, there were the dishes covered in grease from the fried salami. And then there was the sink itself, which needed to be bleached and scrubbed and rinsed until it gleamed.

By three thirty, all that was left to clean were Mother's soiled clothes. They smelled disgusting. If I put the clothes in the sink, the sink would get disgusting. If I put them in the washing machine, the washing machine would get disgusting. I stood exhausted in the kitchen with the bag of clothes, and my heart clenched into a fist. Outside the kitchen window, all the other houses were dark. Inside, mothers and daughters were sleeping in their own rooms, in their own beds with their own blankets that smelled like gentle dreams.

The stench of Mother's clothes curled out of the garbage bag and wiggled its fingers at me. Taunting me. There was no way to clean this. There was no way to be free of it. No matter how hard I tried, no matter how much bleach I used, and no matter how many times I scrubbed, I would never be finished.

But then I remembered.

I was a nomad of the ninth dimension.

I had powers.

I had a backpack full of Necessaries that could dig and cut and slice. I had Letter Opener's smooth blade, Carrot Scraper's tooth, Scissor's claw. I had muscles in my arms, lungs full of magic. I slung the trash bag over my shoulder and tiptoed through the kitchen to the heavy wooden door, where I turned the brass doorknob and pushed. *Quiet. Quiet. Don't wake her up.* And then I was standing barefoot on the porch, bathed in the streetlight. The world was suddenly filled with nighttime sounds. The electric hymn of summer frogs, cicadas, and crickets.

On the side of the house was the old garden shed and the raised patch of ground that used to be a rose garden back in the days when my grandmother made everything bloom. Even though the grass was long and scratchy, the ground was still soft, and it dimpled where I stepped, so I knew this would be a good place to dig.

I unzipped Backpack's mouth and emptied all the Necessaries onto the ground and used them one by one. They all took turns, the soup ladle scooping out dirt, the spatula flinging it, the carrot scraper cutting through roots, and my own fingers plunging deeper and deeper into the hole. Then I found Letter Opener wriggling in the dark. He was so desperate for adventure, he nearly leapt into my hand.

I grabbed him hard by the handle to show him who was boss and used him to slice a rectangle into the earth, three feet long and two feet wide, his sharp blade biting into the ground. When I was finished, I wiped the dirt on the grass and kissed his gleaming blade.

Grave diggers have to work fast. They are ready before the men in suits bring the coffin on its wooden rails, before the family gathers with their heads bowed, each one of them taking their turn to put in a shovelful of earth. The sound of dirt thudding on the top of the coffin, a strange and final drumbeat. When it's over, and everyone has turned their back on the grave and gone home, the grave diggers finish their work. No time to think about who is in there. No time to wonder. Just do your job.

I plunged Letter Opener into the earth. The first cuts were the hardest. We had to get through tangled roots, pieces of clay pots and corners of bricks, rounded stones that used to line the garden beds. I soon figured out that the best way to dig was to use a combination of Letter Opener and my own hands. I used his blade to loosen the earth, and then I scooped up fistfuls of dirt, flinging roots and rocks out of the hole. I used every ounce of energy

I had. I used every muscle in my arms and my back, crouched by the hole, digging furiously.

I don't know at what point I threw Letter Opener aside and started to work at the hole like a dog, scratching with my fingernails, flinging fistfuls of dirt so earth rained over the lawn, all over my hair and my body, scooping with my bare hands until they were raw from ripping out roots. I was dimly aware that I was making noises while I dug. They came from somewhere deep inside me that I didn't even know existed, the sound of my own jagged fury, and my own determination, ripping my voice from my throat until I was weeping while I dug the grave.

I don't know when I realized that I was no longer alone.

I never raised my head or slowed my frenzied digging to see who had come out of nowhere to help me, but at some point, I realized that there was another person crouching next to me with her hands in the grave.

There was another person beside me, crying with me, screaming with me, throwing dirt, grasping rocks and roots, and making the hole deeper and deeper.

I never slowed to see who it was until we were finished. I didn't question it. It was almost as though I had used a spell of transformation and I was so crazed by exertion that I had duplicated and now there were two June Bugs screaming from the pain of earth beneath my fingernails.

And somehow through this effort the grave got deeper, and somehow, finally, it was finished, and one of us flung the garbage bag into the hole, and then somehow we both were on our hands and knees again, covering it up with earth, and then we were patting it down again with our hands and bare feet until there was a mound, and the lawn was covered in dirt, and everything smelled like earth.

We sat side by side by the grave.

"I'm Jenny," said the other person, sticking out her hand like a man.

Her fingernails were black from dirt.

We shook.

"I'm June Bug," I said.

"Yeah," Jenny said. "I know who you are. I've seen you in the neighborhood. You know, your daddy and me, we were best friends when we were kids. He liked burying things too. Maybe it runs in the family."

I looked over at her. I had never seen Jenny this close before. I had always been up in the tree or down the street or behind a window, and she always seemed more like a fairy tale than a real live person. But here she was beside me. Covered in dirt from the grave. That's when I noticed that her left eye was bruised. She had a split lip, and the whole left side of her face was swollen.

"How did you get messed up like that?" I whispered, pointing at her cheek.

She looked at me and frowned. "That ain't polite, asking a person how they got ugly."

"Sorry," I said, looking down at my lap.

"What are you doing digging a hole in your yard at four in the morning?"

"I was burying something."

"Well, is that so?"

"Yes," I said. "That is so."

"Well, we sure made a mess out here. I don't think your mama's going to be too happy when she sees your yard. But then it kind of fits the rest of the disaster your house has become the last few years.

Everything's changed since your daddy and me were kids. When this was your grandma's place, it used to be so pretty. Rosebushes and gardens everywhere."

I looked up at the sinking roof, the dusty windows.

How long had it been since Mother had seen our house from this angle, from the outside, the neighborhood side? Anyone walking down Trowbridge Road could see what I was seeing right now at that very moment: the ivy snaking along the clapboard, the sighing porch sinking to its knees. What on earth is wrong with the people who live in there? Don't they care that it's falling apart? Look at the cracks. Look at the rotting boards. Look at the shingles falling out like loose teeth.

Now there was a new scar. A small, dark grave.

I could see a light on in our bedroom window.

Mother had been awake the whole time.

She had been watching me digging furiously.

She had been watching me weep.

She knew how dirty I was.

There was movement in the window. The silhouette of her head. A thin hand, drawing back the corner of the curtain so she could crouch at the windowsill and peer out at Jenny and me.

I was disgusting from touching the trash bag. I was disgusting from the dirt. I was disgusting from my bad, bad thoughts.

Suddenly I started to cry again.

It was not the uncertain cry of disappointment, or the fleeting cry of something new. This was a wail that had built up over months of watching Mother getting worse, and even further back — to the beginnings of disgustingness and disinfection, the diagnosis and disease. It had Daddy's deathbed in it. It had the black suit he never would have worn, and the blue striped tie Uncle Toby found in the closet. This wasn't my daddy lying still on the white pillows. This was a puppet someone painted to make us believe he was sleeping. At the graveyard, each one of us took turns with the shovel. Each one of us covering the casket with dirt.

I sobbed. I held myself with my dirty hands, and I sobbed and shook.

I grabbed a fistful of dirt and threw it at myself.

I slapped at my arms.

I slapped at my legs.

I shook and shuddered.

"Hey," said Jenny, looking around the street to see if I was waking up any neighbors. "Hey, now.

Shhh, honey. Come on. It'll be okay. You don't want to wake up those Crowley boys, do you?"

Jenny put an arm around me and gave me a few pats, maybe thinking that the gesture would quiet me, but the feeling of a real live mother unraveled me even further, and I wailed like a newborn, opening the dark hole of my mouth and sobbing against her cheek until she pulled me all the way toward her so my head was resting against her, and she held me and held me, wiping the dirt away, saying things mothers say like, "I know. I know. It's over now. It's all over. It's going to be okay."

Jenny Karlo held me a long time on the dirty lawn in front of the grave.

I could see Mother move behind the curtain.

"Look," said Jenny, "your mom's awake. Let's get you inside."

I looked at my filthy hands, my legs and bare feet so covered in dirt, they had turned the color of earth.

"No," I said.

"You can just tell your mama you had a bad dream and sleepwalked out here. Then tomorrow you can go down to the garden store and buy a nice

magnolia or something. Turn this mess into something pretty."

"No," I said again. "I'm not going back in there."

I was surprised at the certainty in my voice, but I
could tell that it was true.

"Are you sure?"

"Yes," I said, shuddering. "I am sure."

Jenny looked at me. "Okay," she said. "Well,
I guess you're coming home with me, then. You
know Nana Jean?"

I nodded.

"I thought you might."

Jenny took my hand. We began walking together
down the quiet sidewalk toward Nana Jean's house,
the stars low in the sky, our shadows stretching
before us from the streetlights.

"Wait a minute," I said.

Jenny stopped short. "You changing your mind?"
she asked me.

"No," I said. "It's just that I forgot my backpack.
It's over there by the grave."

"All right," said Jenny. "Hurry up and get it."

It didn't take long to gather the Necessaries
scattered all around the yard. Tweezers and Carrot

Scraper and Letter Opener. I returned with Backpack swinging on my shoulder. Jenny reached over and took him from me. She hoisted him up onto her back, and we continued walking down Trowbridge Road. "Holy guacamole," she said. "What do you have in here?"

She shook her shoulders. I could hear Letter Opener and Carrot Scraper jangling.

"Oh," I said, trying to sound nonchalant, "just some Necessaries."

"I get it," Jenny said, nodding gravely. "I have Necessaries too."

She opened her purse, took out a pack of cigarettes, shook one onto her hand, found a lighter in her back pocket, and lit up. Jenny took a long drag on the cigarette and then blew smoke over her shoulder. "You asked me what happened to my face before," she said, looking far away. "You still want to know?"

I nodded. "Yes," I said.

"It was a birthday present. From my boyfriend, Donny."

Jenny pantomimed a roundhouse punch.

"That is a really bad present," I said.

"Sure is." Jenny sighed.

She blew a smoke ring into the lightening sky. It drifted like a halo from her lips and hovered over the sidewalk.

"Come on," she said, taking my hand again. "Let's go home."

Breakfast of Champions

Nana Jean always left the house unlocked, so Jenny and I walked right in the back door. I slumped down at the kitchen table and rested my head on my arms while Jenny made us a Breakfast of Champions. She told me this was the only way we would be able to stay awake.

I watched Jenny moving around her mother's kitchen, a grown-up woman with long red hair like a little girl, and wondered what she was like when she was my age, sitting at this table, waiting for Nana

Jean to make her something wonderful to eat. What if she looked like me when she was little, and Nana Jean looked like Jenny, and the world had folded into itself, like two arms of a fan collapsing.

I was expecting the Breakfast of Champions to be food. Orange juice. Bacon and eggs. That kind of thing. But when I saw Jenny taking out a sugar bowl, a jar of honey, a bottle of Coca-Cola, and two tall pottery mugs, I knew I was in for something unusual.

"You're too young for coffee," Jenny said. "But this stuff is better for waking you up than anything I know. Especially if you drink it fast. Your daddy and me, we used to drink these and get so giggly, we'd have Breakfast of Champions coming out of our noses."

She filled our glasses with Coke and scooped ten spoonfuls of sugar and a long dollop of honey into each. Then she stirred them with her finger.

I watched the sugar and honey dissolve into the Coke.

It didn't really bother me that she had her finger in my drink. I was out of Mother's house now. If I wanted to, I could do things that were disgusting right in the open. I could drink something that another person had touched. I could sit at a kitchen table, covered in dirt.

Jenny poured a swig of something from her hip flask into her Breakfast of Champions. Then she gave me a rueful, lopsided smile and raised her mug. "To new beginnings," she said.

I raised my mug. "To new beginnings," I said.

Jenny leaned forward and clinked my mug so hard that the glaze on the pottery chipped, and my cheek got wet from a sugary splash that washed over the side.

I wiped it with my hand and stuck my finger in my mouth. "Mmm," I said. "Tastes so good."

Then I put the mug to my lips and took a tiny sip. Oh my Lord.

Sugar in small doses makes your mouth sing, and it makes your tongue crave more. That's why it's hard to eat just one jelly bean. But Breakfast of Champions was so sweet that even after the first small sip, the inside of my mouth felt like it was coated in syrup.

"Chug it," said Jenny, leaning forward. "You know how? Just tip your head back, open your throat, and swallow as much as you can at one time.

Make it go down fast. I used to make this for Ziggy when he was just a little dude. He could do a whole shot glass in one gulp. Look. I'll show you."

She tipped her head back, closed her eyes, and downed it.

I could see her throat working, once, twice, a third time, and then it was gone.

Jenny started giggling. She pinched her nose a few times, and then wiped her eyes with the back of her hand. "Whew," she said. "Good stuff. Now I'm up."

Jenny twirled around the room, her red hair whipping around her face.

"Okay," said Jenny, when she was done giggling. "Now you do it." She leaned forward across the table and grinned at me. "You were watching, right? Just tip your head back and swallow."

I did what she told me. "Like this?"

"Chug it. Chug it. Chug it," chanted Jenny.

She looked like trouble with the bruise across her cheek and her split lip and all that red hair tumbling down, but I liked it.

I opened my throat, closed my eyes, and swallowed five times. Breakfast of Champions surged through my body, and it gave me such a rush I almost fell off my chair.

Jenny laughed.

I laughed too.

Breakfast of Champions spluttered from my mouth and nose.

My entire body was fizzing, and sugar coated the inside of my throat, making me feel sparkly. I began to spin around because it felt good to be dizzy. Soon Nana Jean's sleepy kitchen was swirling around me. It was the ninth dimension. I didn't know I could get it inside a house. I didn't even know I could get it without Ziggy. But now I knew, I could have the ninth dimension whenever I wanted. All I needed was to chug a Breakfast of Champions.

Jenny threw her arms around me like a best friend, and I was laughing so hard, I thought my heart was going to fly out of my mouth and flutter around the room like a butterfly. I never knew life could be this sweet.

Then Jenny was covering my mouth with one hand and shushing me, because there were sounds from upstairs, then the thumping of footsteps as Nana Jean and Ziggy came stumbling down the stairs, a tumble of sleepy steps as fast as they could muster, and then they were here in the stairwell, blinking at us, not sure if we were real or a part of their dreams.

"Jenny," said Ziggy, wiping his eyes. "Oh, Jenny." Ziggy ran up and threw his arms around her. He hugged her so hard, I thought he might break her, but then I remembered that regular mothers don't break. Jenny stood there for a moment and let him hug her, and then she put her arms around him, closed her eyes, and hugged him back.

Nana Jean stepped forward and took all three of us into her arms. I didn't know how we fit, but we did, a four-way hug, with all of us laughing and crying and rocking back and forth. Ziggy hugging me and Jenny, Jenny hugging me and Ziggy, Nana Jean hugging all of us and wiping dirt from our faces, and Matthew the ferret squirming from one of us to the other, ferreting between our bodies and up onto our shoulders while we rocked like we were doing a huge two-step, like an octopus dancing all around the kitchen.

Somewhere, lifetimes and dimensions and worlds away from Nana Jean's kitchen, I imagine that Mother must still be standing alone at our bedroom window.

How did the glass feel against her skin? Was it smooth and cool?

She would not have opened the window.

She would never have shuffled downstairs in her robe or opened the front door to walk across the street and three houses down. Knock on Nana Jean's door. *I'm sorry, but is my daughter here? It's late, honey, time to come home,* and then take my hand like a mother and walk me back to where I belonged.

Sunrise

———◆———

Morning came like a butterfly unfolding its wings.

We sat at the kitchen table and watched each other yawn. Ziggy put his chin in his hands and gazed at Jenny and at me. Sometimes he pinched himself to make sure he wasn't dreaming, and then Jenny pinched him herself.

Nana Jean smiled the first time Jenny did it, but after the second pinch, she began to look uneasy, and when Jenny reached over to do it a third time,

Nana Jean grabbed her wrist and pulled her close so they were looking face-to-face.

I think if I hadn't been there, she might have said something sharp, but instead Nana Jean touched Jenny's black eye with the back of her finger. Then she sighed, heaved herself up from her chair, made her way to the freezer, and found a bag of frozen peas. She threw it across the room to Jenny, who caught it in one hand.

Jenny leaned back so she was looking at the ceiling with her long legs stretched out. She held the bag on her left eye.

"How did you get the shiner?" Nana Jean asked.

"Donny," said Jenny.

Nana Jean sighed. "I keep telling you that boy is dangerous."

"Only when he drinks," said Jenny.

"Which is all the time," said Nana Jean. "You should have known better."

"Why? I remember one time Daddy gave you a shiner worse than this."

"Please don't bring that up right now," said Nana Jean.

"Why not?"

"Because there are children at this table."

"*I* was a child, Mama."

"Jenny. Please. I love you, honey, but now is not the right time."

Jenny set her jaw hard and looked away. She continued pressing the bag of peas against her eye, dabbing it on the swollen places, wincing when it was tender.

Nana Jean sighed and came to her side. She stroked Jenny's long red hair with her fingers, and even though I could see she was mad, Jenny let her do it. Together, they looked out the window at the garden.

Ziggy rested his head on the table and watched his mother. Outside, the birds were waking up.

Nana Jean went to the window. She opened it wide. There was a breath of wind. The warm smell of soil and vegetables: zucchini, summer squash, string beans, and tomatoes. Now Jenny had tears streaming from her eyes. She didn't even wipe them away.

Ziggy reached over and touched his mother's hand.

"I have a good idea," said Nana Jean, still gazing

outside. "Why don't you and Ziggy go out in the garden and pick me a basket of ripe tomatoes. I think I'll make lasagna tonight."

Jenny didn't say anything. She just looked out the window, the tears coming down.

Ziggy picked up her hand and put it on his cheek.

"Come on, Jenny. The boy needs time alone with you. Let's have a good morning. Later we can talk about Donny. And you can tell me how I was a poor role model, and I can apologize for what you endured when you were little. We can have our very own day of reckoning. Give you a chance to tell me how I messed you up. You'd like that, wouldn't you?"

Jenny looked straight at Nana Jean, her face angry and tight.

"Yep," she said, "I would."

"Well, then, please. Go out in the garden first and get us some good vegetables. They need picking. Otherwise they're going to rot on the vine."

"Let's go," said Ziggy.

Jenny got up from the table.

I shifted in my seat, ready to rise from my chair, but Nana Jean stopped me.

"You stay with me," she said. And when I frowned, she said, "Ziggy and his mama need some time to talk. Let them have some privacy. Meanwhile, you can help me make a good old-fashioned breakfast. After we put some food in our bellies, everything will look less dire. And I sure could use the help cooking. Would you like that, June? Want to help me make breakfast?"

I nodded.

"Good," said Nana Jean.

She took a wicker basket from the counter and handed it to Jenny. "Fill it to the top," she said. "And, Ziggy, don't let that little creature of yours dig around in the garden. I happen to know that this ferret likes gardening almost as much as I do. You just tell him *no* and bop him on the nose if he gets too feisty. Don't be afraid to show him who's boss."

Nana Jean squeezed the nonexistent muscle in his arm.

"Okay," said Ziggy, blushing.

Ziggy reached out for Jenny's hand, and she kissed his hand and took it.

I looked at their two hands clasped together, and something inside me hurt.

"Get going," said Nana Jean. "And, Jenny, when you get back, you and I will have a good long talk about how all of this is my fault."

"Okay," said Jenny. "Thank you."

She held the wicker basket on her hip and swung Ziggy's hand back and forth. They walked together, hand in hand, out the back door and into the garden, the ferret bounding behind them.

The screen door slammed.

Nana Jean and I were alone in the kitchen.

"Ready to help me make breakfast?" she asked.

I nodded.

"Let's get you cleaned up a little bit first. I don't mind a little dirt in my kitchen, but you look like you've been in a war. Anyone ever give you a cat bath?"

"No," I said.

"Well, a cat bath just happens to be the very best way to start off a summer morning. Freshen you right up." Nana Jean took a washcloth and put it under warm water. Then she called me over and told me to sit on a stool. She washed off the dirt with the cloth so gently, like a mama cat licking her kitten. First she knelt in front of me and gently wiped my feet, then my hands. Then my neck, and then my face. Squeezing the brown water into the sink and then putting the cloth back under the warm water until I felt sparkly. "There, now," said Nana Jean. "That's better." A breeze came in through the open window. I could feel it on my face.

"Okay," said Nana Jean, rubbing one more streak off my nose. "Now you're good as new."

"Thank you," I said, suddenly so filled with gratitude that I thought I might burst.

"No need to thank me," said Nana Jean, smiling. "You are about to make me breakfast. So we'll call it even. Let's see how good you are at cracking eggs. There are four of us. I think ten eggs will pretty much do it. And then we'll chop in scallions, mushrooms, spinach, and Swiss cheese. Sound good?"

I nodded.

Nana Jean found a metal bowl, took out a carton of eggs, and set me up by the sink. I started in cracking while she brought berries and bread to the table.

"So," said Nana Jean, gently. "How did you and my Jenny end up back here together?"

The first egg I cracked was perfect. No shell in the bowl at all. I showed the two empty crowns to

Nana Jean and smiled, triumphant. "It's a pretty weird story, actually," I said.

"I can imagine," said Nana Jean.

I cracked another egg and then another. A little piece of the third shell fell into the bowl. A tiny brown shard. I fished it out with my finger. I liked the feeling of the goo on my skin. I put my whole hand into the bowl and wiggled my fingers. The egg whites made my skin feel sparkly.

"Don't do that," said Nana Jean.

She pulled my hand out, wiped it off on her skirt, and then handed me a fork. "Tell me what's going on at home with you and your mama, June. Tell me so I can help."

I kept cracking eggs. When the shell splintered, I fished the pieces out with the fork. Nana Jean showed me the best way to beat eggs. The trick was to move your wrist fast in a circle and to lap at the yolks so they separated and swirled. She held my hand on the fork and guided me. It felt good to have her hand on my hand. I closed my eyes. We stood like that, Nana Jean behind me, reaching around me to hold the bowl on one side and guide my hand on the other. I was surrounded by the warmth of her.

"Tell it," Nana Jean said again. "Just tell it, honey. It's time."

"I don't know where to start."

These were the most honest words I had ever spoken in my entire life.

"Well," said Nana Jean. "How about you start at the beginning."

Golden Boy

———————◆———————

How does anyone tell a story when there are so many beginnings to choose from? My fifth-grade teacher once said that people who write books have to decide which beginning is best. But how could I decide where to start?

This is why at first, I just looked at Nana Jean with my mouth clamped shut, keeping in all the secrets like Daddy used to do. I knew that if I told, it could expose the rotten beams, the crumbling foundation, and, in a single breath, I would destroy everything. How could I tell her that the secrets were what kept us standing on our feet? Every night, we gathered the secrets into our arms and cradled them to sleep. We kissed them on their foreheads. We promised we would protect them.

This is why I didn't even consider telling about the time I lost my tooth and I stayed up late waiting for Daddy to come home from Ryles Jazz Club so I could show him how small it was. It must have been long past midnight because when I woke, the television was all static and snow and everything in the neighborhood was quiet. I woke to the sound of men's voices outside, laughing and shushing each other. I almost didn't recognize one of them as Daddy's. His voice was usually so serious that this new sound of happiness chilled me. I rose with a start and ran to the window.

I could just see them in the shadows, standing together by the garden shed. Here was Daddy and here was a younger man with a guitar case and a brown suede jacket. Daddy was wearing his tweed hat. He had his hand across the young man's mouth, and he was shushing him every time the young man laughed because he didn't want the laugh to wake us up, which was strange because I was already awake and watching them at the window as Daddy leaned back against the shed and the younger man stumbled against him. Then he was moving Daddy's hand from his mouth so that he could get to Daddy's lips. The man held Daddy's face with both hands and kissed him.

It was the first romantic kiss I had ever seen.

Of course, I had seen grown-ups kiss before. Mother and Daddy kissed every once in a while. There was tenderness between them. But this was something different. I stood wide-eyed at the window, amazed by the way they held each other and by the way they smiled and looked into each other's faces.

But then Daddy looked at his watch and stepped away.

"I have to go," he said. "My wife and daughter are in there waiting for me."

"I know," said the young man.

"I'm sorry," said Daddy.

"No," said the young man. "Please don't be sorry."

There was silence.

They held each other's hands. Then the young man turned away and walked across the lawn with his guitar case. I could hear a car door close.

Then Daddy walked alone to the porch. He sat down on the wooden swing for a while, leaning back with the fedora tipped over his eyes, and pushed himself with his feet, back and forth, back and forth, looking up at the porch ceiling with its peeling paint and its cobwebs.

I tiptoed back to the couch and curled on my side. I covered my head with the pink quilt and pretended to be asleep. Minutes passed. Finally, the screen door opened and closed. Daddy's footsteps shuffled into the room. I heard him take off his coat and the tweed hat and hang them on the coat rack. The floorboards creaked, and there was the familiar everyday sound of Daddy sighing. Then silence. Everything in the room was still. Was he looking at my muffled form pretending to be asleep beneath the quilt? Was he staring up the stairs to the bedroom where Mother slept alone? Did he see our house with brand-new eyes tonight: the parlor with its scalloped chairs and white lace curtains, the study filled with bookshelves and sheet music, the photographs that showed the three of us, a family, posing with our arms around one another.

Daddy came over to the couch and sank down by my curled feet. He reached over and stroked me.

I could feel his hand on the quilt, rubbing my legs, patting my back in circles the way he used to do when I was a little baby, and then the warmth of his body bending down and kissing the very top of my head. That kiss still lingered when he gathered me in his arms, quilt and all. He carried me against him, a happy bundle, all the way up the stairs to my very own bedroom, where he laid me down on my pink bed and kissed my eyelids, one and then the other.

"Daddy," I muttered, pretending to wake up.

"Shhh," he said. "Go back to sleep, my lovely love."

"Daddy, I lost my tooth today."

I opened my lips and poked my tongue through the space in my teeth.

"Oh my goodness," he said. "Congratulations, baby."

"I was brave," I told him, sleepily, yawning into the darkness. "I yanked it out all by myself."

"Oh, you yanked it, did you?"

"Yes," I said. "And it bled and bled. All over my mouth and my chin and my shirt. Mother had to clean me. She didn't like that."

"No," he said. "I wouldn't think she'd like that very much at all."

"I stayed up. I wanted to show you," I said, yawning. "I wanted to show you how brave I was."

"You *are* my brave girl," he said. And he kissed my forehead again.

Then he walked over and sat on the rocking chair, leaned his head back, and rocked while I rubbed my cheek into the pillow.

Little by little, I drifted back into the kind of sleep only a very little girl can feel when her daddy is sitting in her rocking chair, in her bedroom, watching over her, and loving her every second as she sinks deeper into sleep. He was still there when I turned on to my side and hugged my pillow into my heart, and he was still there when the first morning's light streamed in through the lace curtains, so that the very first sight I saw when I woke the next morning was Daddy's sleeping face, his head leaning back against the rocking chair, his eyes and cheeks streaked with shadows.

Summer Baskets

Ziggy and Jenny proceeded into the kitchen with a basket overflowing with ripe summer vegetables. When they presented it on the wooden farm table, it looked like a painting with the early-morning sun glazing the curved surface of the tomatoes. There was a thick bouquet of kale flowing over the side of the basket, so rich in summer's juice, I imagined I could see blood pulsing inside each stalk.

Ziggy drummed on the kitchen table with

fingers spread wide. Jenny bowed and began to dec-
orate herself with vegetables. She threaded scallions
through each of her buttonholes, and tied marigold
stems into her hair. Then she twisted pea pod vines
around Ziggy's wrists and smeared raspberry juice
across his cheeks like war paint.

"Huzzah," said Ziggy. "Enter the fairies in their
veil of vegetable sunshine."

"That's my boy," said Jenny.

She took Ziggy's hands and swung him around
the kitchen, laughing hysterically.

What would it be like to have a mother who
decorated herself with vegetables and smeared raspberry war paint on my cheeks?

I tried to imagine Mother dancing me around
the kitchen, but I couldn't. Uncle Toby, yes, but
never Mother. When I tried to imagine Mother's
face smiling as wide as Jenny's, head thrown back,
all those teeth showing, all I could imagine was a
nightmare.

"I missed you so much," said Ziggy.

"Oh, Ziggy," said Jenny. "I missed you too."

Ziggy and Jenny waltzed around the kitchen.

I was a stranger. I didn't belong here. I didn't
belong anywhere.

I swayed on my feet, but Nana Jean steadied me.

"Easy there," said Nana Jean, putting her arm around me. "Honey, it's time to tell me what's going on so I can help. Look at you, baby. You're shaking. I can't help you unless you tell me. Okay, darling? We'll have some breakfast together. And then we're going to try again. That sound okay with you?"

I nodded, wiping my eyes with the back of my hand.

Ziggy and Jenny twirled and dipped and held hands. They kissed each other's cheeks and laughed and laughed.

I stood with Nana Jean by the kitchen table and swallowed my jealousy.

Ziggy and Jenny jumped on chairs, raised their faces to the ceiling, and howled like wolves.

Nana Jean frowned.

"Ziggy. Jenny. You stop this. How do you think this girl feels watching the two of you carry on like this? June Bug, honey, these two here, they are just *really* happy to see each other. But all of us are glad that June Bug Jordan is with us here this morning, aren't we? Makes the reunion even more special. Isn't that right, Jenny? Ziggy? See? They're glad you're with us. Please, let's think for a moment before we do any more strange things that exclude someone. Let's remember all the hard times we've been through. All of us."

Nana Jean went to the table and helped them down. When Jenny started to twirl again, Nana Jean clamped one hand on her shoulder.

"Jenny," she said.

"What?" said Jenny.

"Set the table for breakfast, please. You know where everything is. China plates, please. And Grandma's silver. June Bug here is making a delicious breakfast, and we need to celebrate being together on this special day. Make some good memories before things get hard again. Now, June, why don't you come to the stove and help me do the last step? It'll just take a minute and then we can eat. We'll feel more settled after we get some food in us. And then you and I have some serious talking to do."

"What about me, Mama?" said Jenny. "You and me have some talking to do too."

"Jenny," said Nana Jean. "If you want to tell me about how I ruined your life, surely it can wait until after breakfast. I'll listen to you, I promise. I'll even agree with you. But I think I'll keep my humor much better with some breakfast inside me first. So, could we wait awhile, please? After breakfast, we can all have a good talk and a good cry. Okay? June Bug first. Then you."

"Okay," said Jenny.

"Okay," I whispered.

Nana Jean put her arm around me and led me back to the stove, where we turned on the burner, melted the butter, and then poured the eggs into the pan. They sizzled and sputtered. Nana Jean held my hand on the wooden spoon and helped me stir up the eggs so they were fluffy and gorgeous.

"Take a breath through your nose," said Nana Jean. "What kinds of spices does it need?"

I leaned forward and took a long sniff. I almost fainted, it was so wonderful.

Nana Jean brought over some fresh dill and the salt and pepper shakers.

"You season this any way you want, June Bug," she said.

I sniffed through my nose again. Then I crumbled up some dill and shook in three shakes of salt and three shakes of pepper.

"Perfect," said Nana Jean.

Ziggy and Jenny got out the silver and the good

china and set the table. Matthew scrambled down Ziggy's leg, up the table, and squirmed his way into the basket of vegetables. He curled up beside the eggplant, chirring faintly before settling into sleep. He tucked his nose beneath his tail and closed his eyes. No one seemed to mind. Especially since he looked so lovely next to the curved black hip of the eggplant.

There is something wonderful about sitting at a kitchen table for breakfast. You find your chair, lower yourself down, pull into the table. Maybe you spread your napkin across your knees, a happy white square. The sun shines differently in the morning. Things are still fresh.

We pulled in our chairs, and Nana Jean came over with the skillet. She heaped eggs onto our plates and then sat down herself. The chair creaked under her weight.

I speared a huge forkful and brought it to my watering mouth, but Nana Jean stopped me with a sharp look.

"We have to say grace," said Ziggy.

I put my fork down.

"Jenny," said Nana Jean, "why don't you say grace? It's been a long time since you prayed at this table. I think the good Lord will appreciate hearing your voice instead of mine, for a change."

"Okay," said Jenny. "But only if you let me do it my own way."

"Honey," said Nana Jean, "you do everything in your own way. Why would this be any different?"

Jenny reached her hands out to either side of her. Nana Jean took one and Ziggy took the other. For a moment I was jealous that no one was holding my hands, but then, sure enough, Nana Jean reached out to hold my hand on the left and Ziggy reached out to hold my other hand on the right. We sat that way for a few seconds, just feeling each other's presence around the table. A few seconds is such a tiny amount of time, but it can feel enormous when you have someone's skin next to your skin and the smell of eggs on the table steaming in the new morning sun.

"Dear Lord," said Jenny, "we thank thee for these here scrumptious gifts we are about to receive, these super-duper delicious breakfast eggs that our new friend, June Bug Jordan, from down the street, hath made for us."

Ziggy smiled at me.

"I think you know June Bug Jordan, Lord. You

sure knew her daddy a long time ago when he used to come over here and play with me, on account of me praying so much that he would one day be my husband.

"Does he play music for you up in heaven? Mama used to have an old Hammond organ down in the basement, and he'd come after school to sing hymns to me. You remember that, don't you, Lord? I'd bring down my blanket and my dolls, and I'd lie right down on the floor to listen. Sometimes I'd get tired and fall asleep, but that's okay 'cause when you fall asleep listening to hymns, you dream about angels.

"Folks said if he'd ever liked girls at all, we would have made a good-looking couple. Everyone thought so. Bet he would've treated me better than drunk old Donny."

"Jenny," said Nana Jean, "remember that this is a prayer, please."

"I'm doing this my own way, Mama. You said I could."

"We agreed that we would have this conversation after breakfast."

"This isn't a conversation, Mama. This is a prayer to the Lord."

"God help us," muttered Nana Jean.

"Dear Lord, you know I used to hear Mama and Daddy at night. Sometimes I'd hear her crying. Where were you when that happened, Lord? What about when Daddy went on his last bender and drove his car into that big old tree out front? Can't say things got better after he left us. But they sure did get quieter."

"Jenny," said Nana Jean. "Please. Say 'Amen,' and let's be done with this."

"I am not done," said Jenny. "I'm still thanking the Lord for all our gifts. So, as I was saying, thank you, Lord, for taking Daddy when you did. Thank you for sending me Marty. He was a good friend, even if he never did love me.

"We sure were surprised when he came back from that fancy conservatory with June Bug's mama on his arm. Were you there at their wedding? That weird, somber affair? You know I wished them well, Lord, you know I did, even though everyone could tell that it was not going to end well."

"Jenny," said Nana Jean. "This is cruel."

But it didn't feel cruel to me. I listened with a hunger for the truth that rivaled my hunger for the eggs that were cooling on my plate, and I reached out for every word, grasping at them, bringing them toward me, tasting them, rolling them in my mouth, devouring them, digesting them, and then reaching out for more.

"Were you at his funeral, Lord? Did you see June Bug and her mama, holding hands up front? They didn't know I was in the back, praying for them. I was. Because I knew they were gonna miss that man something awful. I knew June Bug lost her daddy and Angela Jordan lost her husband, even if they couldn't have had much of a romantic love like most husbands and wives are supposed to. I have no idea how many times they did what they needed to do. All I know is somehow this beautiful little June Bug was born. Sometime along the way, Angela and Marty must have learned what I learned with Donny. If you give a person enough wine and turn off enough lights, everything gets easier. Just close your eyes and imagine whoever you want to imagine. That's what I did when Donny took me home. I just closed my eyes. Pretended he was someone gentle like Marty. Pretended he was singing hymns to me. Velvety and gorgeous for all eternity. Amen."

"Amen," said Ziggy.

They stared at each other across the table.

"That was inappropriate on so many levels I don't know where to begin," said Nana Jean.

"I am your child, Mama. I learned everything I know from you."

"You didn't need to drag these children into it."

"They're already in it, Mama. For God's sakes, it's their story."

Ziggy took a bite of eggs and looked into my eyes. "These are wonderful eggs," he said.

"Thank you," I muttered.

I ate my eggs in silence. They tasted good.

Ziggy was right. There was just the right amount of pepper and salt. And the eggs were perfect and fluffy. We sat around the table and swallowed the truths Jenny had told in her prayer. I could tell Nana Jean was mad. And I could tell one of the reasons she was mad was because she thought it hurt me to know these things about Daddy. But it didn't hurt. It was a beautiful prayer. This was the first time in my life I had ever heard anyone tell the truth about who I was and what I came from.

And now I knew another truth too. A daughter

can tell her story and the house can stay standing and the floor can stay whole. A daughter can tell the truth and a mother can listen. And so can God. The foundation beneath their feet might shake, but it will not crumble. The floor will not open up to swallow them. Now I knew that a mother and daughter could be angry at each other. They could be furious. They could even hate each other for minutes or even sometimes years. But then they could sit at the kitchen table together on a sunny morning and eat breakfast, and they could swallow the food and feel full.

When breakfast was over, we helped Nana Jean clean up. Ziggy brought the dishes from the table to the counter. Jenny washed them in the sink with warm water and soap. My job was to dry them with a soft blue washcloth, a simple task, but one that I discovered was perfect for me, because I loved wiping away the water to find a clean, round surface shining underneath.

Nana Jean brought the dry dishes to the china cabinet. Every time I handed her a plate or a bowl, she made sure to touch me before taking it, squeezing my arm or petting my hair. Sometimes she just looked at my face, gentle and apologetic.

When the dishes were finished, Nana Jean came up to me and put her arm around my shoulders. She walked me through the kitchen to the living room. The windows were open and there was a breeze blowing through. I wondered if Daddy ever sat in this room with Jenny. I wondered if he loved it the way I loved it just then.

"Are you doing all right?" Nana Jean asked me.

"Yes," I said. "I'm doing fine."

Nana Jean smelled like talcum powder, and the skin on her arm was soft as rising bread.

I leaned into her.

"I wanted to apologize for Jenny," she said.

"You don't have to apologize," I said. "It's okay."

"It's not okay," said Nana Jean, her face serious. "Not at all." She sighed. "It's not an excuse, what I'm going to tell you, but my Jenny, she dealt with a lot of hard things when she was a little girl. She just doesn't know what's right and wrong sometimes. I'm glad you're not feeling too angry or hurt about what she said. But I tell you, I sure am shaking from it."

I closed my eyes, leaned my cheek against her shoulder, and took a breath through my nose. Oven biscuits. Blueberry muffins. Popovers.

"Poor child," said Nana Jean. "You've got enough on your mind, without adding my daughter's revelations to them."

We sat side by side on the sofa, looking through the tall windows onto Trowbridge Road. Mr. Delmato was mowing his lawn across the street. Mrs. Wright was standing on her steps with a watering can. She was giving her geraniums a drink. The Crowley boys were riding back and forth on their bicycles.

We watched the neighborhood outside the window. The same porches, and the same pretty children ducking in and out, slamming screen doors, moving between the houses in small ragtag tribes. It was the same neighborhood, but somehow it seemed different now.

The wind moved through the living room, stirring the lace curtains like gossamer.

Nana Jean slipped off her shoes and put her feet up on the coffee table.

We sat together in silence.

I think she knew I was going to tell even before I did.

Otherwise she would have made some kind of small talk about the weather or the neighborhood, or urged me into some kind of activity, handing me a pillow or offering me something to eat or drink, giving me something to hold in my hands, but she didn't do any of these things. She just sat beside me and waited patiently. Her silence was gigantic and extraordinary. It brought the poison up from my blood to the surface, where it burned and begged to be released.

Outside the window, the Crowley boys continued to ride their bicycles back and forth in front of their houses. The mailman came and Mr. Koning went out to get it. They talked at the doorstep. The mailman tipped his hat. Mr. Koning waved. The truck made its way down the street. You would have thought, looking out that window at the way the neighborhood went about its business, that no one else in the world had secrets.

They knew the right things to do and say. They knew when to wave and when to close their doors and go inside to their troubles. But somehow they went on. Sometimes they cracked like Mother did.

Sometimes they were not able to bear it. But most of the time they found some way to live. Even Jenny and Nana Jean. Even with all that hurt inside.

I took a very deep breath. "Nana Jean," I said.

"Yes, baby," she said, reaching over to squeeze my hand.

"I want Ziggy and Jenny to be here when I tell."

"Okay," said Nana Jean. "I'll get them."

She heaved herself from the couch and shuffled back into the kitchen. I could hear her whispering to them, and then, slowly, she brought Ziggy and Jenny in from the kitchen.

Jenny sat in the old rocking chair and leaned her head back. Ziggy sat at my feet.

He put Matthew on my lap.

Nana Jean sat next to me and put her arm around me.

No one said anything. They waited for me to find my courage.

"I have something I want to tell all of you," I said, finally.

Truth

Sometimes I spoke out loud. Sometimes I spoke in a whisper. Sometimes I spoke with almost no sound at all, especially when it seemed that using my voice might make the truth grow gigantic like a monster coming to swallow us whole, reaching out with hairy fingers and a snaggle-toothed grin. Sometimes I glanced at Nana Jean to see if she was shaken by what I was saying, but mostly I just looked out the window or down at my lap at Matthew and told.

Nana Jean kept her eyes on me so that she could catch all the words or read my lips when I was too quiet to hear. I told things I had never said out loud.

How Mother had never been easy in the world, even before Daddy got sick.

How she always had demons that would scrape at her brain with a sharp finger, picking at her thoughts as though they were scabs that kept growing back and then bleeding again.

How once she woke in the middle of the night, convinced that the cramp in her foot was a splinter that had become infected, and how she would check her foot and check her foot and check her foot, and ask and ask and ask Daddy if he thought a person could die of a splinter.

People sometimes die of splinters, don't they?

No. I don't think so.

But how can you be sure?

I just am.

Are you completely sure or just a little bit sure?

Completely sure.

Are you just saying that to make me stop?

No. I really mean it, sweetheart.

What if you're wrong?

I'm not wrong.

If you're wrong, I could die of this splinter.

You are not going to die.

But the splinter has been in there for five months.

I'm pretty sure there's nothing there.

What if it's just too small to see?

No. If it were there, I'd see it. I have always had excellent eyes.

Are you sure?

Yes. Yes, I am.

Are you completely sure, or just a little bit sure?

Oh God, Angela. Completely sure. A thousand percent sure.

There is no such thing as a thousand percent. You are ridiculing me.

Honey. There is nothing in your foot. Please. Stop this. I can't stand it.

Daddy had called it her *artistic temperament.* This is why she had the determination to practice one phrase of one movement of one piece over and over again until it was right. Practicing was the only way to smooth the tangles, to brush out the lines so that no stray hairs sprang out: one note that was too sharp, a shift that knocked into the fingerboard. All imperfections had to be polished away before a piece was ready to perform.

"You two are my saviors," Mother told us before her concert at Carnegie Hall. "What would I do without my two angels to protect me?"

Were we really her angels?

It is true that we tiptoed around her quiet sanctuary. We knew all the rules. We knew how to leave our shoes by the doorstep. We knew how to recognize the bad days without asking. If it was already ten o'clock and Mother had not yet gotten out of bed, it meant that the demons were loud today and we had better get out of the house and let Mother wrestle with them on her own.

On really bad days, when the demons were so loud even I could almost hear them, Daddy would take me to Hyde School playground and push me on a swing so high, I would imagine I was a bird flying over all of Newton Highlands, over the trees, over Crystal Lake, over the tall houses with the wind in my feathers. Sometimes, we would clink three round quarters into the toll box and the trolley man would let us ride from Newton Highlands to Copley, and then from Copley onto the E line, and from the E line to the art museum. We would spend the afternoon wandering through galleries, holding hands, making up stories about the portraits. *This one's name is Moe. His favorite thing to eat is ice cream.*

The first time Mother's sanctuary splintered was the very same day the serious nurse told us the news, her face blank and expressionless. *No one knows very much about it. We do know that he will get worse. And eventually he will die. We also know it is very contagious. You and your daughter will need to be careful.*

Suddenly there was the question of bodily fluids. We didn't know what was okay to touch and what wasn't. All we knew was it was inside him and it was going to make him sick and eventually it was going to kill him. The serious nurse gave us pamphlets that first day: *What You Need to Know about AIDS.* That's when Mother decided I should stop holding hands with him. If I fell and skinned my knee, instead of Daddy blowing on my cut three times like he used to, *puff puff puff,* and then kissing it and patting down the bandage, I should start caring for my cuts and scrapes by myself.

You're a big girl now, June Bug, said Mother.

I was a big girl. Old enough to know that my age wasn't the real reason I had to bandage my own cuts. If he touched an open wound, maybe I would catch it too, and what would Mother do with both her angels gone? It would just be too horrible. Too horrible to even imagine.

I think you're taking things too far, Angela. No one said I couldn't touch her. Nothing's going to happen if I just touch her.

How do you know?

I just know. I don't have any open sores on my skin.

A sore can be tiny.

Not that tiny. I would feel it. I would see it. And then if I had one, if I actually had a sore on my hands, I would wear gloves. If I had a sore in my mouth, I could wear a face mask. But honey. Please. June Bug needs me to be her father. You have to allow me to get near her while I'm still okay. Otherwise you'll have to start doing all the things I've been doing around here. Can't you see that?

I'll need to learn how to do them anyway. When you're gone, I'll be all she has left.

You are going to need to touch her. Even if it's a bad day.

I know, Marty. Don't you think I know?

Even if you're feeling horrible. Even if you wake up in the morning and you're feeling really bad. It won't matter. Angela. You'll have to be the one to touch the food

and the shoes and the cuts and scrapes and everything.
How's that going to work? Have you thought about that?

I'll make it work. What's our choice?

There was no choice.

Daddy went from looking well to looking sick. His body was covered in dark blotches. He lost so much weight that we could see his bones pushing up beneath his skin. And then there were the sores and the horrible stomach cramps and what came out of them. This is when Uncle Toby became our messenger. He brought us groceries and picked me up from school.

That's when Mother started closing off rooms, shutting doors, making the house into a smaller, more manageable space. There were sick rooms and there were well rooms. I was not allowed to go into any of the sick rooms. Daddy was not allowed to go into any of the well rooms. We called to each other up and down the stairs. We knocked secret codes on the walls. Mother brought Daddy his meals on paper plates and Styrofoam cups, and he would eat with plastic forks, knives, and spoons, so that when he was finished eating she could throw it all away.

The only one who was allowed to move between the sick rooms and the well rooms was Mother, who began wearing latex gloves and a face mask inside the house. In the final weeks, she would sit in the dining room, where we kept Daddy's hospital bed. She would play Bach suites for him. When the cramps were bad, she would walk him to the bathroom, one slippered foot at a time. She would change his bedding and then burn the sheets.

It's okay, Mother called from his sick room, *just turn your face away and breathe through your mouth until I'm done cleaning him up. But, please, don't touch anything.* Then, when Daddy was clean and sleeping, she climbed the stairs to our bathroom. She filled the tub with scalding water and Clorox bleach, and she submerged herself up to her chin so that the next time she touched me, she would have no trace of AIDS on her skin.

The routine became almost impossible in the final days, when there were lots more accidents, and lots more soiled sheets. There was also more calling back and forth from the sick rooms to the well rooms as we tried to exist in our separate worlds.

I'm hungry. It's time for lunch. When are you making me lunch?

June, Daddy isn't feeling well right now. Please. Make something yourself.

You never cook for me anymore.

Honey. Please. Your hands are clean. Make yourself a sandwich. Uncle Toby brought over some peanut butter and jelly, and there's white bread on the counter.

I don't know how to make a sandwich.

That's ridiculous. Of course you know how.

I'm going to starve. If you don't make me something, I'm just going to starve.

Okay. Starve, then.

The sound of Daddy weeping. The toilet flushing. Mother's voice, speaking low to him, almost too quiet to hear from the well rooms, where I was safe and far away from his dying.

"Is that when she stopped feeding you?" Ziggy asked me.

I nodded, tears streaming down my face.

"As a punishment?" Ziggy asked in anger and disbelief. "You wanted her to be your mama, but she wanted you to go away and leave her alone. So she never fed you again as long as you lived. She let you starve to death. The end."

I nodded, tears streaming down my cheeks.

"You should have made the sandwich," said Jenny.

"Jenny!" said Nana Jean.

"It was my fault," I said. "After Daddy died, she wouldn't go outside anymore. She stopped bringing me to school. Everything was disgusting to her. Everything can kill us. Dirt or germs or anything outside. And now whenever she thinks I'm contaminated, she gives me a disinfection bath and makes me clean again."

"What is a disinfection bath?" Ziggy asked.

I lifted up my shirt and showed them how my skin had become white and wrinkled. I showed them the places where the burns had become scars.

"Dear God," said Nana Jean.

"You should have made the sandwich," said Jenny, with tears in her eyes. "If you had only made the sandwich, things would be fine. You kids don't know how good you have it."

"No," said Nana Jean. Then she turned to me. "Honey, it wasn't your fault. Please know that. Nothing that happened is your fault. And I don't think your mama stopped acting like a mother because she wanted to punish you. She just got too sad and broken is all. When Marty was dying, and then after he passed, she just got too sad, and too overwhelmed, and probably too angry at the world to give you what you needed, honey. And pretty soon, I think, she just couldn't handle thinking much about anything except those demons of hers. It was never about you. It was about her."

"Are you sure?" I asked Nana Jean with a quavering voice.

"Oh, yes, sweet child. I am absolutely sure."

"But what if you're wrong?" The question rose into the air like smoke, and I thought I could hear a note in my voice that sounded like Mother.

"June Bug, I am not wrong about this."

Nana Jean reached over and held both my hands.

"Do you think my mother is a bad person?"

There was a long silence.

Jenny and Nana Jean looked at each other.

"Do you?" whispered Ziggy, almost unable to bear it.

"Do you?" Jenny asked.

Nana Jean took a very deep breath. She reached out and touched her daughter's cheek.

"No," she said, looking into Jenny's eyes. "I just think she wasn't ready for what was going to happen to her. I think she tried as hard as she could to handle what life put in her path, and then she just kind of broke."

"Oh, Mama," said Jenny. "Oh, Mama, thank you."

"Thank you," I whispered.

"Don't thank me," Nana Jean said. "Please, honey. Don't thank me."

Aftermath

With all those truths ringing out in the open air, everything felt raw and strange. No one talked for a while. My story swirled around the room, the way sometimes when you've been spinning in circles a long time, even once you've stopped, you can still feel the world moving. Jenny went into the kitchen for the frozen peas. She came back, lay down on the couch, and pressed the cold plastic bag across her forehead and closed her eyes.

Nana Jean swung into action. She hauled out

the phone book and started turning pages. "Got to keep you safe," she said. "We all have to do the right thing, sweet girl, even when the right thing is hard. I'm going to call someone about what you just told me. Then I'm going to call your mama. And then I'll tell you what we're going to do next, okay?"

"Okay," I whispered. "Are they going to come and take me away?"

"No one is taking anyone away," said Nana Jean. "These are just phone calls. And then we'll talk."

"Are they going to put my mother in jail?"

Nana Jean stopped and looked me full in the face.

"Whatever happens next will be the right thing for you and your mama. I promise."

"But what *is* the right thing?"

"I don't know," said Nana Jean, honestly. "I don't know, sweet girl. But I'm going to find out. Now I need you kids out of the house for a while. I have something important I got to do now, okay? And I need to be able to think."

I didn't move or speak. My heart was beating too hard.

"Okay," said Ziggy. "If you need us, we'll be outside."

Nana Jean picked up the phone and began dialing.

I went to get Backpack from the kitchen. Ziggy put Matthew on his head. We left Jenny and Nana Jean in the living room, and we walked slowly, side by side, out of the living room, down the front hallway, out the door, down the porch steps, and over to the copper beech tree, where the sun was shining through the leaves.

How could the sun be shining when everything in my life was changing so fast?

I climbed the tree with Backpack on my shoulders. Ziggy went next with Matthew on his head. I put out my hand and helped him up. We looked at each other's faces.

"I think Nana Jean is going to call the police," I said.

"Me too," said Ziggy.

"Do you think they're going to take my mother away and put me in foster care?"

"I don't know," said Ziggy. "Maybe."

"Maybe they'll let me stay with you and Jenny and Nana Jean."

"You could be my sister."

"Yeah," I said. "We could be a family."

But we both heard the way those words rang in the air, and we could tell it wasn't going to be true.

I took Backpack off my shoulders and placed him between us.

"Will you help me keep my balance while I do something really important?" I asked Ziggy.

"Anything," said Ziggy. But his voice was breaking.

"I'm going to carve my name into this tree," I said. "So when they take me away, there will be part of me left behind."

"Don't talk that way," Ziggy said.

"I don't want you to forget who I am."

"How could I forget you?" said Ziggy. "You have been my first true friend."

"And you have been mine," I said. "Help me turn around so I can face the trunk."

Ziggy steadied himself by hugging the branch with his knees. He reached out and held my waist, leaning into me and pulling down while I inched around so my cheek was leaning against the trunk. Once I found a smooth spot with no burls or notches, I began my work.

"First I need Letter Opener," I told him.

I could hear the clatter of Necessaries behind me. Ziggy handed me Letter Opener by the wooden handle.

I pushed on his flat blade to chip into the bark, clearing away the skin. I worked until I had chipped away a small, neat square. I chiseled Letter Opener back and forth until the bark fell away. I knew it hurt to rip the tree's flesh. All scars hurt. But maybe pain was the right thing to remember that once upon a time there was a girl named June Bug whose mother loved her, but didn't how to make it stick.

"Okay, Ziggy. I'm handing back Letter Opener now. Just put him back in and be careful not to cut yourself. He's sharp."

"All right," said Ziggy, his voice small and shaking. "I'm ready."

I handed him back nice and slow.

"What do you need next?"

"Scissors," I said. "He's at the bottom somewhere."

There was the sound of Necessaries clattering as Ziggy fished around inside Backpack.

Ziggy handed Scissors to me, and I took him.

I used Scissors to carve each letter of my name.

With the tough bark gone, the wood was soft. It was easy to drag his long tooth into the patch. I started with the *J*, a long, curved loop and then a straight edge. Then the *U*, deep and curling. The *N* and the *E* were the hardest, with three and four separate slices. Once I had the outline of each letter, I traced inside each groove, pressing the blade over and over again until the cut of each letter was deep, about a quarter of an inch into the flesh. Now I could see my name clearly. Each letter bold and clear, announcing my name to the neighborhood for the first and last time. *Ladies and gentlemen, I present to you JUNE JORDAN. Remember her.*

I handed back Scissors.

"Now give me Carrot Scraper, please."

There was the sound of clattering Necessaries, and then Ziggy handed Carrot Scraper to me. I used Carrot Scraper's pointy tip to carve thin, feathery spiderweb lines all around my name, etching radiating waves from each letter to the scarred edge where flesh met bark again. Now there were snowflake lines radiating from each tip of the *J*, from the two arms of the *U*, from each arrowhead point of the *N*, and from every waving finger of the *E*. Then I started to carve designs into the frame, digging tiny nicks all along the fleshy patch. Nick. Nick. Nick. All around. So that if you looked hard, it looked like my name was trying to shine like a diamond.

"It's beautiful," said Ziggy.

"Now it's your turn to make ZIGGY so you can leave something behind too."

"I don't think so," said Ziggy. "I'm not going anywhere."

"But Jenny came back for you. Maybe tomorrow or the next day you'll be going home."

"She didn't come back for me," said Ziggy. "She came back because of her eye. She'll stay until the swelling goes down. And then she'll go back to Donny."

"How do you know?"

"That's what she did the last time," said Ziggy.

"Maybe this time will be different."

"Maybe," said Ziggy. "But I'm not going to hold my breath. Besides, Nana Jean said that the house on Trowbridge Road can be mine as long as I need it to be. And I think that's pretty good, all things considered."

"I guess you're right," I said.

But deep down inside, I wasn't sure anything was better than your very own home.

I tried to imagine what it would be like to live somewhere new. I tried to imagine a place without rules for staying clean or closed rooms or secrets. I tried to imagine a place without bleach baths or locked doors. Then I tried to imagine resting my head on some other pillow in some other place without Mother smothering me, without her scent or the sound of her cello. I tried to imagine someone else saying *June Bug* first thing in the morning when the new sun was shining. I tried to imagine a new mommy who would make me soup when I was hungry and dry the rain off my face after a storm, then tuck me into my very own bed when I was too tired to stand. At first I felt hopeful, imagining this new place. Then I felt heartbroken. And then I felt so bewildered and confused that I could barely see straight. I began to shake.

"Hey," said Ziggy. "Are you okay?"

"I don't know," I said.

I clutched the branch and tried to breathe.

"Do you want to get down?"

I looked at the ground. It seemed so far away.

I nodded, clutching the branch.

"Want to go to Majestica?"

I nodded again.

"Okay," said Ziggy. "I'll help you."

Ziggy started down first just a few steps in front of me so he could help me if I slipped. He put his hands on my feet to keep me steady, guiding me silently when I couldn't find the right place to step. I kept my eyes wide open. My feet slipped from the footholds, and my hands didn't know where to grasp. Close to the bottom, I froze in the middle of a step like Mother frozen at the threshold between the stairway and the kitchen. I froze and shook, suddenly terrified for my feet to slip, but Ziggy guided me gently, one inch at a time, until I was standing on the ground.

I was on my own two feet again. I was so exhausted and so thankful that I almost wanted to sink to my knees and weep, but Ziggy reached out and put his arm around my shoulder. He smiled his crooked, lopsided smile so full of sadness and friendship that I had no choice but to smile back, even though my heart was breaking.

Wings

———◆———

Make-believe is a kind of real magic. Make-believe can change a cellar hole into a sanctuary. It can change a ferret into a dragon. It can turn the cawing of crows into a choir of angels.

Ziggy took Matthew from his head and put him down in the leaves. The ferret bounded down the hill into the ninth dimension, unaware that anything was about to change, his four feet racing, back arched high until he reached the bottom, where he spun in circles. We could see flashes of white when his head and tail peeked from the leaves.

Ziggy and I walked down the hill. I took Backpack off beside Majestica. We climbed into the hole. The sun was shining through the spaces between the sticks, casting golden rays of light into the shadows.

We smoothed the quilt over the leaves and rested our heads on the pillow.

Once upon a time, the farmer and his wife rested their small white heads on their musty feather pillows and slept the sleep of the old. The farmer got up early and milked the cows and worked in the fields, and the farmer's wife kept the fire going in the wintertime and kept the kids fed and the clothes mended. Sometimes there were dragons, and sometimes there were crows, and sometimes there was thunder and lightning, and sometimes the farm was full of beasts that hid in the shadows and only came out after it rained.

I tried to take it all in. I tried to memorize each stone, each leaf, the handle of the water jug, the railroad nail, the black leather sole of an old boot, the clay marble, the piece of petrified coal, the old glass bottles.

"I'll miss this," I said.

"Please don't talk that way," said Ziggy.

"I never got to sleep here," I said. "I never got to really and truly live here."

"You have always lived here," said Ziggy.

"Even when it was a farm?"

"Even then," said Ziggy. "Even before it was a farm when it was a forest, and even before that, before human beings existed, when there was such a thing as dragons."

"I want to go back there," I told him. "Just one last time."

"Me too," said Ziggy.

"Let's change into dragons together."

"Want to do it at the same time?" Ziggy asked me.

"Yes. At exactly the same moment."

"Okay," said Ziggy. "Should I count to three?"

"No," I said. "I can do it. One. Two. Three."

We grew so quickly, we had to struggle out of Majestica so that we didn't break it open with our gigantic wings unfurling.

Ziggy was a flaming-red dragon. He stood on the earth and breathed fire. I could hear the rumbling fire work its way into his chest, and out of his gleaming jaws as he pushed off with his powerful back legs and rose into the air, flapping his wings to coast above the clouds. His fire made the sky glow red.

I allowed myself to grow and grow until I was enormous. I rose into the air with my dazzling black wings that extended over the neighborhood, and when I spread them, I darkened the sky. Summer cooled in an instant. I blew air through my lips, and a slow, freezing fire billowed out onto the earth. Suddenly there was frost on each blade of grass.

The tiny red dragon snorted his warning. He was alarmed. He lashed his tail and gestured for me to descend.

I smiled a dark, frigid smile. I twisted and twirled. The entire neighborhood spun into my vortex, the houses and trees and neighbors and cars and dogs on their leashes, and the shops down on Lincoln Street all ripped from their foundations, and everything slurped into my hungry mouth, and I was rising so high above the clouds and growing so gigantic that the earth was just a small blue lozenge that I shoved into my mouth, tucked into the corner of my cheek. It was sweet and filled with disappointment and bravery and heartbreak and love.

The tiny red dragon cowered between the clouds. He shivered and buried his head in his wings, but I loved him, so I spared him his life and slurped him into my mouth along with the universe so I did not hear when he began to pray that I show him mercy and that I show mercy to the entire earth, which rattled against my teeth like a tiny blue bead.

It wasn't a matter of mercy, of course. It was a matter of hunger. I wanted to consume everything I saw, to swallow the universe and hold it inside like a baby all safe and protected, floating inside me, wiggling its toes and fingers. I swooped through space and sang it lullabies. I rocked my belly and smiled while it fell asleep. What does the universe dream about when it is sleeping? It dreams about being fed. It dreams about leaning back on pillows while angels drop grapes into its mouth. It dreams about a tongue running over the surface of that grape and then the flood of sweetness, galaxies spiraling into space.

Then I began to hear a small, wheedling voice from deep down inside my belly.

Hey!

Hey, June Bug!

It was the red dragon who had turned back into Ziggy.

I slowed my wings and my frenzy. I stopped the universe from spinning.

June Bug!

I opened my mouth and breathed fire. I let the earth and the moon jump out. I breathed out oceans and stars. I breathed out Ziggy.

Then I slowed my black wings and became small enough to fit inside the universe. I could see the earth down there, a beautiful gleaming marble.

Ziggy was waving to me. He was a tiny speck of perfection so far below, I almost couldn't see him.

I let myself drop.

Whirling down to earth. Not too fast. Riding the solar thermals down. Drifting.

Then I landed and became June Bug Jordan again.

Ziggy was lying in the grass next to Majestica.

I lay down next to him.

We gazed at the clouds.

Matthew danced after butterflies.

"That was nice," said Ziggy.

I smiled. There were tears in my eyes. But I felt warm and full.

We lay on our backs and let the earth reassemble around us.

That is when we started to smell the smoke.

It was rising from somewhere on Trowbridge Road.

We could see it rising.

"What's that?" Ziggy asked me, breathing in through his nose.

"Did *we* do that?"

"I don't know," said Ziggy.

"I didn't mean to do that," I said, my heart lurching.

"Of course you didn't."

"I was just playing."

"I know," said Ziggy.

"It was make-believe."

We heard the sound of sirens.

"They're coming for me."

More sirens.

"They're going to bring me to jail."

Voices calling back and forth along the street.

The smell of smoke.

Resurrection

———◆———

I barely remember climbing down into the darkness
to hide. I barely remember Ziggy wrapping the quilt
around my shoulders or lying down beside me in
the leaves, police sirens and fire trucks and ambu-
lances wailing into the neighborhood. They must
have called our names for hours, frenzied voices
we would have recognized if we had not been
paralyzed. I don't remember falling asleep, but if I
could have created a dream for myself, I would have

dreamed about dragons and crows. I would have dreamed about a farmer and his wife and the moon outside their window. I would have dreamed about beasts that hide in shadows and a man in a patchwork coat and a woman with a cello playing desperate apologies into the smoke as the sun went down.

There were voices on the hill. Hurried. Strained. Footsteps. Screaming. "Over here!"

"Hurry!"

Ziggy still had his arms around me. His face was buried in my hair, and when I turned, I saw that his cheeks were smeared with dirt. Ziggy pushed my tangled hair back behind my ear and wrapped the quilt tighter around my shoulders. We sat up and blinked. Ziggy wiped a smudge of dirt from my cheek and leaned his warm head against my head. We sat and breathed. Then more footsteps above and someone was hurling the branches from Majestica. It was Uncle Toby.

"Oh, thank goodness!" he cried. "June Bug! Ziggy! You're okay! Oh, thank God! Nana Jean! Come over here! I've found them! They're both okay!"

Uncle Toby kicked away the branches until Majestica was just a cellar hole again. The plain gray fieldstones were covered in broken bottles and pieces of trash. There was a torn quilt and a ratty pillow. We were exposed. Uncle Toby climbed into the hole. He took my face in his hands. "Are you okay?" he asked. I nodded silently, almost imperceptibly. "Are you okay?" he asked Ziggy. Ziggy nodded too. And now Uncle Toby had his arms around us, and he was rubbing the dirt from our cheeks and pulling leaves from our hair and kissing our heads and helping us out of the cellar hole and back into the world.

Nana Jean was there to receive us with fresh blankets. She made that keening sound that only a grandmother can make, that mixture of happiness and terrible sadness and relief and elation and despair, and she pulled us close to her body and hugged us like she wanted to pull us safe inside. I closed my eyes and let myself be enveloped by her. The scent of roses and talcum powder and smoke.

"I'm sorry," I said. "I'm so sorry."

"Oh, honey," she said. "You have nothing to be sorry for. None of this is your fault."

"It is," I said. "I turned into a dragon and breathed fire. I wasn't careful. All I wanted to do was fly."

"You didn't do this," said Uncle Toby. "It was Angela. The firefighters said it started in the kitchen and then it spread. Wood burns fast in an old house."

"It started in our kitchen?"

"That's what they said."

"She was cooking something?"

"I don't know," said Uncle Toby. "Maybe."

"I called her on the phone a few hours before it happened," said Nana Jean, speaking carefully, as though the words could hurt me. "I told her you were staying with me, and that you were safe and you loved her, and she seemed so relieved to hear it, honey. But I had to tell her the truth. I had to tell her that you had explained to me about how things had been going for the two of you, and I told her that I had called someone. She said she didn't want anyone coming over to talk with her. She said she wanted to be left alone."

Ziggy reached over and took my hand.

"The firefighters have been looking for you for hours," said Uncle Toby, crying openly now. "We thought you might have gone back there looking for her. We thought you might have gotten trapped inside somehow. But then Buzz and John-John said we might find you here. They said this is where you like to play, and we might as well check to see. You know something strange? I used to play here with your daddy and Jenny sometimes too. We used to look for old bottles in the leaves and make-believe all kinds of things. Oh my goodness. To find you here of all places. And both of you all in one piece. It's like a miracle."

He took me from Nana Jean and hugged me for himself.

"I knew things weren't right," he whispered into my hair. "I knew your mom was sick. But I didn't realize how bad it was. Why didn't you tell me?"

"I didn't want to make you worry," I said.

I buried my head in his T-shirt. His heart was beating. It was gentle like my daddy's heart. It knew what kind of sadness lived inside that house, even before there was such a thing as AIDS. It knew what happens to a person when they hold on to secrets for too long, or what happens to a home when it becomes a holding place for those secrets. It crumbles. It burns.

"Is the house gone?" I asked.

"It's gone," whispered Uncle Toby.

"The whole thing?"

"The whole thing," said Uncle Toby.

"And Mother?"

Nana Jean held Ziggy close.

Uncle Toby let out a long, shuddering sigh and looked me right in the eye.

"They got her out," he said. "They took her to Saint Elizabeth's. They are going to treat her burns first. And then they are going to work on treating the rest of her. The doctor said that sometimes folks need to hit rock bottom before they begin to heal. I don't think there's a lower bottom than this. But she's going to get help, June Bug. She's finally going to get the help she needs."

I sank to my knees in relief. Toby sank down with me to hold me, and Nana Jean and Ziggy came to put their arms around us. They knelt in the pine needles with us, and we all cried for a good long time until there was nothing left inside us. Nana Jean helped us up. We were all so tired and sad and relieved, we were swaying on our feet. We had to hold each other to stay upright.

"Come on," said Nana Jean. "It's been a long, horrible day. The police are going to want to talk with you soon and find out more about what's been happening with you and your mama. Let's all go back to my house and get cleaned up and have something to eat before they come."

"I'm not hungry," I said.

"Of course not," said Nana Jean. "But let's go, anyway. Maybe we can find a minute or two to breathe before life plays its next trick."

"Is Jenny at home waiting for me?" Ziggy asked, his voice small and hopeful.

"She sure is," said Nana Jean. "She wanted to stay put just in case you came back looking for us. She is going to be so relieved that you are safe, Ziggy. She's been worried sick about you."

"She has?"

"Of course she has," said Nana Jean. "She loves you more than anything else in the whole wide world."

Nana Jean put her arm around Ziggy, and they started up the hill to the house.

Uncle Toby and I followed behind. Every few steps or so, he stopped and kissed the top of my head and pushed my hair behind my ears and wiped the dirt and tears from my face. He gazed at me and kissed me and then made himself keep going. I leaned my head into his shoulder. His T-shirt smelled like smoke. He put his arm around me, and we walked slowly, slowly, back up the hill, past Nana Jean's boxwoods, through the orchard and then the garden.

Jenny was waiting for us on the back porch, and when she saw Ziggy, she came running. She must have been full of sorry for what she did and didn't do. But it was clear that Nana Jean was right. She loved him something fierce, even though she didn't always know how to make it stick. I could tell by the way she whirled him around and around and clapped his cheeks and rubbed his nose with her nose and kissed his forehead and pulled him into the house, screeching for joy.

Nana Jean stood alone on the back porch.

She took a deep, shaking breath, leaned one hand against the door a minute, smoothed out her skirt, squared her shoulders, and followed them inside.

Uncle Toby and I stood in the garden. The whole world smelled like smoke, but underneath you could still smell the late-summer tomatoes and the good brown earth. We didn't go in for a while. We just stood in the garden together with our arms around each other. But pretty soon there was another smell: bread baking in the oven. Something stirred deep inside me. Something that wanted to live.

"Maybe I will have something to eat," I said.

"Whatever you want," said Uncle Toby, rubbing my back. "Whatever feels good and whatever you need you should do. You've been through so much. I can't even imagine."

I looked at his face. He had long eyelashes like Daddy. His eyes were so full of worry and love and sadness that it almost broke me open.

I didn't know what to do so I hugged him, and he hugged me back.

His arms were strong. They held me close.

"Uncle Toby," I said.

"Yes, June Bug?"

"Can I live with you while Mother is in the hospital?"

"Would you like that?"

"Yes," I said. "I would."

"I would like that too."

"And you won't ever give up on me?"

"Never," said Uncle Toby. "You're all I've got."

"You're all I've got too."

"I don't know about that," said Uncle Toby. "You have your mama. And it also seems to me you have some very good friends in there who love you something fierce. Life can put mountains in your path that seem too high for anyone to climb. But you have all these people who love you, June Bug. And that's got to count for something."

I leaned into him and let him support me. I put my arm around his back, and he put his arm around my shoulders and helped me walk out of the garden, up the back steps, and into Nana Jean's kitchen, where there was fresh-baked bread on the counter and a long table with chairs already set for us, and the last rays of the setting sun slanting light across the old wooden table like an angel spreading its wings.

Something New

It was a tiny apartment, he said. Right in the center of town, right above the grocery store. He set it up for about a week, moving furniture and boxes while I stayed behind with Ziggy, Jenny, and Nana Jean. One evening Jenny had an announcement to make. She told us she had given it some serious thought and decided she would move back home to live with Nana Jean for good so all three of them could live together and start over the right way this time, which made Ziggy so happy he howled like a wolf.

Nana Jean made us ravioli and Italian wedding

soup, and salads from the garden. She brushed my hair and gave me cat baths. In the afternoons, Ziggy and I wandered around the garden. Sometimes we climbed the copper beech tree. Sometimes we climbed down into Majestica. Neither of us felt much like transforming. Our worlds had changed enough in one summer to last a lifetime. At night Nana Jean helped me to telephone Mother in her hospital room. Her voice sounded faint and far away, but there was something new inside it I hadn't heard for a long, long time. Something that sounded just a little bit like hope.

Then one day, just a week before we started school, Uncle Toby said everything was ready for me. I kissed Nana Jean goodbye and gave Ziggy and Jenny the best high slide I knew how. They waved goodbye while Uncle Toby and I walked together from Trowbridge Road to Chester and from Chester to Lincoln Street. It was an apartment above the grocery store in a row of brick buildings that all had shops on the bottom floor and apartments on the top. Behind the building, I saw a skinny cat dart quick as a shadow behind the trash cans before Uncle Toby told me it was time to go on up, so we opened the lock and let ourselves in, and we walked up the one, two, three flights of narrow steps that wound past the supply room, past the grocery office, and up, up to the very top floor, where there was a green door that was all ours. Uncle Toby handed me one key, and I turned it in the bottom lock. Then he handed me another key, and I turned it in the top lock. Then I pushed hard with both hands.

It was dark inside.

"Just a minute," said Uncle Toby, brushing past me. "Let me turn on the light."

I stayed in the doorway until the light went on. Then I stepped inside.

On one side of the room, there was an over-stuffed leather couch, kind of beat up but comfy, all covered with pillows. There were a couple of armchairs with patches on the arms and a red and orange rag rug so our feet would never be cold on the hardwood floor. In the back, there was a kitchenette with yellow and orange counters and a yellow stove and sink and a neat yellow fridge that was a little smaller than our fridge on Trowbridge Road had been, but not too small for all the good food inside that Uncle Toby said he would always and forever feed me whenever I was hungry: orange juice and cheese and celery and carrots and apples and peaches and eggs and milk and brown bread and all different kinds of cold cuts, and a packet of chicken thighs and a packet of hamburger, and a bag of marshmallows and all kinds of yogurts in colorful cups. Inside the kitchenette, there was a little alcove with a scratched-up table and two mismatched wooden chairs, one for Uncle Toby and one for me.

"Do you like it?" Uncle Toby asked me.

I nodded, but I wasn't completely sure.

I sat down on one of the kitchen chairs. It was a little wobbly, but it was good enough for me, and I could gaze out the little window that overlooked Lincoln Street. I could see all the stores down there and all the cars and people coming and going. I could see the post office and the pizza place and the barbershop and the drugstore. The sun was getting ready to set and the sky in Newton Highlands had that hazy blush you only get at the end of the summer when it is hot and dry. A last gasp of fever before autumn makes everything crisp.

"I know it looks a little rough around the edges," said Uncle Toby, wiping a hand across the scratched table and turning around to gesture to the couch and the chairs. "And it's going to take some time getting used to something so small after all those years on Trowbridge Road." He put both of his hands on my shoulders. "But it's only a few blocks away from Nana Jean's house. Just a few blocks away from the school. You and Ziggy can meet on the corner and walk together. And we can visit him any time you'd like. I think you and I are going to be happy here."

We looked out the window together. There was a mother and a daughter walking a little white dog. They both had ice-cream cones, and the girl was dancing around and licking her ice cream, her ponytail flipping one way and the other while she danced, and the little white dog was barking from all the excitement, jumping up on her and wagging his tail the way only small dogs can do. The mother was lovely and laughing, making sure the leash didn't wrap around her daughter's legs, and when she was bending down, her ice cream fell on the ground, and the little white dog dove right in and licked it up, wagging his tail so hard it looked like a blur. We watched the mother and the daughter wait on the sidewalk for the dog to finish. Then the daughter put her arm around her mother's waist and the mother put her arm around the daughter's shoulders, and they walked slowly together, their footsteps keeping time, all the way down Lincoln

Street, mother and daughter sharing one ice cream, the dog trotting along at their heels.

I put my hand on the window and watched them go.

"Come on, June Bug," said Uncle Toby. "I want to show you your bedroom."

"I have my own?"

"Of course," said Uncle Toby. "And it's all set up for you. Don't you want to see?"

"Yes," I told him.

He took me past the little bathroom and the linen closet to the two white doors on either side of the hall that led to our two separate bedrooms.

"This one is mine," said Uncle Toby. He opened his door and I could see a futon, shelves made of milk crates, and his guitar case propped on one side of his bed, erupting with scribbled sheet music. His window was all set up with wine bottles that had different colored candles with wax melted all along the edges. "It's kind of a mess already," he said. "But that's the way I like things. If that bothers you, I can keep it picked up."

"No," I told him. "That's okay."

He opened my bedroom door and then took a step back so I could go in first.

There was a pink quilt on a white four-poster bed, all stitched with tiny roses and vines. There was a pink ruffled pillow and pink curtains, and there was a little white desk with an old-fashioned lamp with an embroidered white lace shade. On the desk there was a photograph.

"Go on," said Uncle Toby. "Look and see what it is."

It was a close-up of Mother holding me when I was just a newborn. You could see my round bald head and my round pink cheeks and one closed, feathered eyelid. Daddy was next to Mother on one side, with his arms around her, and Grandma was on the other side, and you could see all three faces glowing and gazing down at me and smiling these enormous smiles. There was nothing forced. Nothing held back. No secrets. Just love. Just pure, unquestionable love.

"I took that picture at the house on Trowbridge Road," said Uncle Toby, "the day your mother and daddy brought you home from the hospital. You asked me one time if I thought they loved each other. Just look at that picture, June. Look at their faces. If that isn't love, I don't know what love is."

I touched the picture of my father's face. It was a moment of happiness.

"He had a secret," I said to Uncle Toby. "He had a secret he kept his whole entire life."

"I know," said Uncle Toby. He put his arm around me. "But if it makes you feel any better, it wasn't a very well-kept secret. Everyone who knew your daddy knew that he loved men."

"But you said he loved my mother."

"He did," said Uncle Toby. "You only had to see them to know that too. But maybe it was a different kind of love. I don't know. People are just complicated, I guess. I think we have room for all kinds of love in our hearts. That's why Nana Jean can love Ziggy so much and that's why I can love you. And that's why I think even though things are hard right now for both of us, I really do think that it is all going to be okay."

I hugged the photograph next to my heart. Then I kissed each face, Mother's, Daddy's, Grandma's, and mine, and then I put the photograph back on the desk and angled it toward the bed so tonight when I go to sleep, I could look at all those faces loving me and remember.

"Uncle Toby?" I asked.

"Yes?"

"Can we go to the ice-cream store and get me an ice-cream cone?"

"We sure can," said Uncle Toby.

"I want strawberry with chocolate sprinkles."

"You got it," said Uncle Toby.

"And, Uncle Toby?" I asked.

"Yes?"

"Can we share the ice-cream cone?"

"Sure," said Uncle Toby. "But you can have your own if you want."

"No," I said. "I want to share it with you."

"Okay," said Uncle Toby. "One strawberry ice-cream cone to share coming right up."

"Can we leave the light on while we're out so it's not so dark when we head back up?"

"Sure," said Uncle Toby. "We can leave the light on."

Outside, the sun was going down. There was a breeze, and the heat was bearable for the first time all day. The ice-cream store was right on the corner, next to our building. We walked in together, past the kids twirling around on their blue and red stools.

Uncle Toby ordered us a double-scoop strawberry ice-cream cone with chocolate sprinkles, and the man behind the counter scooped it into the cone, twirled it into the sprinkles, and handed it to him. "Nice night for an ice cream," he said.

"Sure is," said Uncle Toby, putting a dollar and two shiny round quarters into the man's open hand. "We just moved into an apartment in the building next door. I have a feeling we'll be getting a lot of ice-cream cones."

"Well, I'll make sure to have a lot of strawberry on hand, then. Welcome to the neighborhood."

We thanked him and walked outside.

The sky was the color of pink roses.

"Uncle Toby?"

"Yes?"

"Do you think tomorrow we can invite Ziggy out for ice cream?"

"Sure," said Uncle Toby.

"And, Uncle Toby?"

"Yes?"

"Can me and Ziggy share a strawberry ice-cream cone if it's okay with him?"

"I don't see why not. When we get home, we can call him and make a plan. Would you like that?"

"Yes," I say. "I would like that very much."

There was the hum of the cicadas. A faint stirring of wind across our bare arms.

"Can we walk down the street a little before going home?" I asked.

"Of course," said Uncle Toby.

I put my arm around his waist, he put his arm around my shoulders, and we walked down Lincoln Street together, passing our ice cream back and forth, not saying much, just walking slowly as the late August sun dipped behind the brick buildings on Lincoln Street, the sky blushing tentative and hopeful as it dimmed into evening.

Author's Note

In 1983, when *Trowbridge Road* takes place, the virus we now know as HIV had just been identified. Most people were learning about AIDS for the first time, and their behavior toward those who received the diagnosis was often based on fear, prejudice, and misinformation. We now know a lot more about prevention and treatment of HIV than we did back then. Today, thanks to medical advancements, AIDS kills fewer people, and men and women with the virus can live long, full lives. If Angela Jordan had understood the disease as we do now, Marty could have spent his final days surrounded by family, and June Bug could have continued getting hugs and kisses from the father she loved until the very end. In some ways, Angela's battle with mental illness, both during and after Marty's disease, was just as destructive as AIDS was in their home, because her illness prevented the family from making the connections they needed to feel sheltered and nourished by one another, especially in a time of need.

If you or a family member is suffering from mental illness, please do not struggle alone. Reach out to someone you trust—a family member, a friend, a teacher, or a counselor—and tell them you are hurting. For more information and support, please visit the website of the National Alliance on Mental Illness at nami.org or call their hotline at 800-950-NAMI. Your voice is important. No one should have to suffer in secret.

Acknowledgments

This book would never have seen the light of day if it weren't for all the people I love who believed that June Bug had important things to say and that young readers needed to hear her voice. Thanks to my beloved husband, Steve, who read every draft with the kindest eyes, and who sighed and smiled in all the right places; to Joshua Andreas and Benjamin Kasiel, who took my hands and led me down the mountain in the dark; to Sally Brady, Esther Ehrlich, Lester Laminack, and Ken Harvey, who read early drafts and offered wisdom and support; and to my beloved agent, Victoria Wells Arms from HSG Agency, for believing in me and in this book. You always knew that at its center, *Trowbridge Road* was really about love. Finally, I wish to send my most enormous gratitude to my editor Liz Bicknell at Candlewick Press for her vision, her humor, her certainty, and her remarkable artistic trust. You gave me the courage I needed to fly from earth to the ninth dimension and back again.